二版

超簡單 手繪旅遊英語

Tourist English With Pictures

作者 Iris Chang
繪圖 橋本友紀
審訂 Dennis Le Boeuf／景黎明

目 錄

Part 1 基本

❶ Numbers （數字）…… 10
❷ Units of Measurement （測量單位）…… 12
❸ Time （○點○分）…… 14
❹ Dates（○月○日）…… 16
❺ Days, Weeks and Years （星期與其他時間）…… 18
❻ Time Periods（期間）…… 20

Part 2 招呼語

❼ Greetings/Saying Goodbye （招呼語）…… 22
❽ Introduction （介紹）…… 24
❾ Request and Help（請求幫助）…… 26
❿ Weather and Seasons （天氣與季節）…… 28

Part 3 機場、機內

⓫ Inside the Airport 1 （機場內 1）…… 30
⓬ Inside the Airport 2 （機場內 2）…… 32
⓭ Airports and Airlines （機場／航空公司）…… 34
⓮ Immigration Procedures （入境）…… 36
⓯ During the Flight （機艙內）…… 38

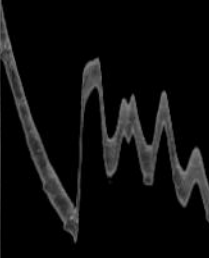

Part 4 交通

⑯ Traffic （交通） 40
⑰ Train Station 1 （車站 1） 42
⑱ Train Station 2 （車站 2） 43
⑲ Buying Tickets （買車票） 44
⑳ Taking the Train 1 （搭乘火車或捷運 1） 46
㉑ Taking the Train 2 （搭乘火車或捷運 2） 48
㉒ Taking the Bus / Taking a Taxi （搭乘公車／計程車） 50
㉓ Renting a Car 1 （租車 1） 52
㉔ Renting a Car 2 （租車 2） 54
㉕ Driving a Car （開車） 56
㉖ Filling Up the Tank （加油） 57

Part 5 飯店

㉗ In a Hotel 1 （飯店 1） 58
㉘ In a Hotel 2 （飯店 2） 60
㉙ Problems and Complaints （飯店內的糾紛） 62
㉚ Service and Facilities （飯店內使用的單字） 64
㉛ Hotel Services （飯店內的服務） 66

Part 6 購物

㉜ Shopping（商店）………… 68
㉝ Shopping for Clothes and Shoes（購買衣物基本會話）………… 70
㉞ Shopping Mall（購物中心）………… 72
㉟ Fitting 1（試穿 1）………… 74
㊱ Fitting 2（試穿 2）………… 76
㊲ Looking for Product Information（尋找商品）………… 78
㊳ Shopping for Cosmetics（化妝品）………… 80
㊴ Convenience Store（便利商店）………… 82
㊵ Electrical Appliance（電器用品）………… 84
㊶ Payment（付帳）………… 86

Part 7 飲食

㊷ Eating and Drinking 1（用餐基本會話 1）………… 88
㊸ Eating and Drinking 2（用餐基本會話 2）………… 90
㊹ Tableware（餐具）………… 92
㊺ Food Flavors（味道）………… 94
㊻ Fast Food（速食）………… 96
㊼ Japanese Bar（居酒屋）………… 98
㊽ Drinks（飲料）………… 100
㊾ Asian Food 1（亞洲食物 1）………… 102
㊿ Asian Food 2（亞洲食物 2）………… 104
51 Hot Pot（火鍋）………… 106

52 Chinese Common Dishes（其他常見料理）........ 107
53 Soups and Appetizers（湯品與配菜）........ 108
54 Sushi（壽司）........ 110
55 Western Style Food（西餐）........ 112
56 Coffee / Tea（咖啡／茶）........ 114
57 Desserts（甜點）........ 116
58 Fruits（水果）........ 117
59 Seasoning（調味料）........ 118
60 Special Request on Food（特別要求）........ 120
61 Dining（飲食）........ 122

Part 8 觀光

62 Asking for Directions 1（問路 1）........ 124
63 Asking for Directions 2（問路 2）........ 126
64 Holidays and Festivals（節慶假日）........ 128
65 Christmas（聖誕節）........ 130
66 Baseball（看棒球）........ 132
67 Amusement Park（遊樂園）........ 134
68 Zoo（動物園）........ 136
69 Aquarium（水族館）........ 138
70 Religious Buildings（教堂與寺廟）........ 140
71 Hot Spring（溫泉）........ 142
72 Galleries / Museums（美術館／博物館）........ 144
73 Outdoor Activities（戶外活動）........ 146

Part 9 日常生活

74 Making Phone Calls 1（打電話 1）…… 148
75 Making Phone Calls 2（打電話 2）…… 150
76 Mail System（郵局業務）…… 152
77 Bank（銀行）…… 154
78 Currency Exchange 1（兌換外幣 1）…… 156
79 Currency Exchange 2（兌換外幣 2）…… 158
80 ATM …… 160
81 Laundry（洗衣店）…… 162
82 Hair Salon（美容院）…… 163
83 Fixing Items（修理物品）…… 164
84 Lost and Found（遺失物品）…… 165

Part 10 事故、糾紛

85 Traffic Accident（交通事故）…… 166
86 Car Problems（汽車故障）…… 168
87 Having Trouble 1（遇上麻煩 1）…… 170
88 Having Trouble 2（遇上麻煩 2）…… 172

Part 11 生病就醫

89 Illness（常發生疾病症狀）…… 174
90 Body Parts（身體部位名稱）…… 176

91 Injury & First-Aid （受傷與急救） 177
92 Body Parts and Organs（手、內臟及其他身體部位） 178
93 Skin Disease / Common Disease （皮膚／其他疾病） 179
94 Medical Care （疾病／受傷時的說法） 180
95 Medication （藥物） 181
96 Other Diseases （其他疾病） 182
97 Medicine （醫療相關字詞） 183

Part 12 人際社交

98 Self-Introduction （自我介紹） 184
99 Occupation （職業） 186
100 Hobby （興趣） 188
101 Sports （運動） 190
102 Daily Conversation （社交談話） 192
103 Blood Types / Astrological Signs （血型／星座） 194
104 Chinese Star Sign （十二生肖） 195
105 Personality （性格） 196
106 House Types （住屋） 198
107 Music （歌唱與音樂） 200
108 Opposite Words （反義詞） 202

附錄：出國點檢表 —— 205

前言

本書是完全針對初學英語的讀者所設計的旅遊英語書籍，以出國旅遊會遇到的情境為主，全書採手繪方式表現，內容輕鬆活潑，易於閱讀。

全書分為 12 大主題，從最基本的應用單字到平日的食衣住行、會話應對，全部包含其中，讀者可針對需要的主題練習單字及會話，不必學習多年的英語也能與人溝通。

除旅遊必備的單字及對話外，作者也在部分章節補充相關資訊，讓讀者在外出旅遊的同時，也能獲得實用的旅遊常識。

本書使用說明

全書內容以手繪彩圖呈現，理解最快，
閱讀最有效率，記憶最輕鬆！

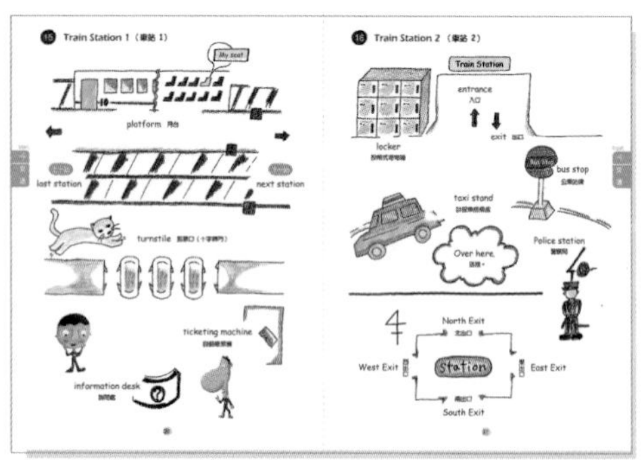

針對各種旅遊情境列出實用的例句與單字，
也可直接套用例句，現學現用、琅琅上口！

36 Fitting 2（試穿 2）MP3

Can I see the [ ] in the display case?
我可以看一下展示在櫃裡的 [ ] 嗎？

tie 領帶	clip earrings 夾式耳環
scarf 圍巾	pierced earrings 穿洞式耳環
shawl 披肩；圍巾	necklace 項鍊

配合主題補充實用資訊，不必花時間
查詢必要的資訊！

由國外撥打電話回台灣，如：（02）2365-9739。

國際冠碼	+國碼	+區域號碼	+對方的電話號碼
如 001（美國）或 000（法國）	886（台灣）	2（區域號碼的「0」要去掉）	2365-9739

1. 一般電話可利用上述方法直接撥電話回台灣。
2. 利用行動電話撥回台灣，則要看機種。有的不能撥打，有的是與電話公司簽好合約後就可以撥打。
3. 利用公共電話撥打時，要看清楚該機是否可打國際電話，並需購買國際電話卡。

Part 1 基本

1 Numbers（數字） MP3 1

1	2	4	5
one	two	four	five
6	7	9	10
six	seven	nine	ten

11	12	14
eleven	twelve	fourteen
16	19	20
sixteen	nineteen	twenty

30	40	50	60	70
thirty	forty	fifty	sixty	seventy
80	90	91	46	73
eighty	ninety	ninety-one	forty-six	seventy-three

100	200	300	400
one hundred	two hundred	three hundred	four hundred

314
three hundred (and) fourteen

730
seven hundred (and) thirty

Example

1,000 one thousand

2,000 two thousand

10,000 ten thousand

30,000 thirty thousand

A : How much does it cost?
= How much is it?

B : US $ 7,500.

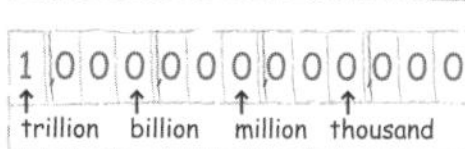

1,000,000（百萬） (one) million

1,000,000,000（十億）
(one) billion

1,000,000,000,000（一兆）
(one) trillion

1/2 half 1/4 quarter

30%
thirty percent

5.1
five point one

Cardinal Numbers and Ordinal Numbers 基數與序數

基數（Cardinal Numbers）是用於表示數量的數字，如：

one、two、three、forty、nineteen eighty-six (1986)

序數（Ordinal Numbers）用於說明順序的數字，提到日期、樓層、名次等有「順序」的說法時，就會使用到序數。

序數的說法

1st first	2nd second	3rd third	4th fourth	5th fifth
6th sixth	7th seventh	8th eighth	9th ninth	10th tenth
11th eleventh	12th twelfth	15th fifteenth	18th eighteenth	
21st twenty-first	22nd twenty-second	23rd twenty-third		
24th twenty-fourth				

- first choice 第一選擇
- second child 第二個孩子

樓 層

一 樓 the first floor	二 樓 the second floor	五 樓 the fifth floor

- The vegetarian restaurant is on the 3rd floor of this building. 素食餐廳在本棟三樓。

2 Units of Measurement（測量單位）

MP3 2

Part 1 基本

I'll take a pair of ice skates.
我要買一雙溜冰鞋。

an apple 一顆蘋果	a battery 一顆電池
an eraser 一個橡皮擦	a backpack 一個背包

- a glass of tap water
  一杯自來水
- a cup of coffee
  一杯咖啡
- a cup of black tea
  一杯紅茶
- a (glass of) beer
  一杯啤酒
- a bottle of wine
  一瓶葡萄酒

a piece of clothing 一件衣物	two pair(s) of pants 兩條褲子
a bunch of roses 一束玫瑰花	a briefcase of cash 一箱現金

Two cups of coffee, please.
請給我兩杯咖啡。

cm centimeter 公分	m meter 公尺	km kilometer 公里	g gram 公克
kg kilogram 公斤	ml milliliter 毫升	l liter 公升	

Useful Expressions 常用小對話

1. Bartender: What can I get you? 要喝點什麼？
   Customer: I'll have a whisky on the rocks. 我要一杯威士忌加冰塊。

2. Sales assistant: What is your waist measurement? 你的腰圍是多少？
   Customer: I have a twenty-six-inch waist. 我的腰圍26吋。

3. The airport is two kilometers away. 機場離這裡兩公里遠。

4. It's a 6-volt rechargeable battery. 這是一個六伏特的充電電池。

電壓的換算

常出國旅遊的人一定知道，許多歐美國家的電壓與我們所用的並不相同，因此如果要自行攜帶電器，別忘了先查詢各國的電壓，多帶一個變壓器（transformer）或電壓轉換器（voltage converter）。以下為各國的電壓：

國名	電壓 V	國名	電壓 V	國名	電壓 V
台灣	110	美國,加拿大	120	紐西蘭,香港 德國,法國 荷蘭,中國	220
日本	100	英國,澳洲	240		

英制（Imperial Units）與公制（International System of Units）換算

	1 m 公尺	1 yd 碼	1 ft 呎	1 in 英吋
yard 碼	1.094			
foot 呎	3.281	3		
inch 英吋	39.37		12	
cm 公分	100			2.54

	1 kg 公斤	1 lb 磅	1 oz/ounce 盎司
pound 磅	2.205		
oz/ounce 盎司		16	
kg 公斤		0.454	
1 g 公克			28.3495

3 Time（○點○分）

MP3 3

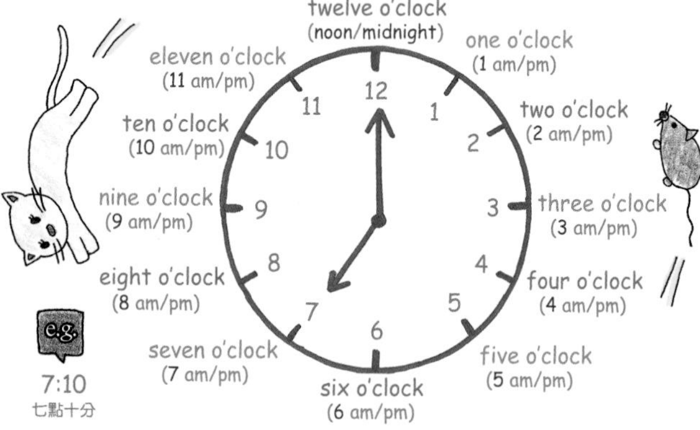

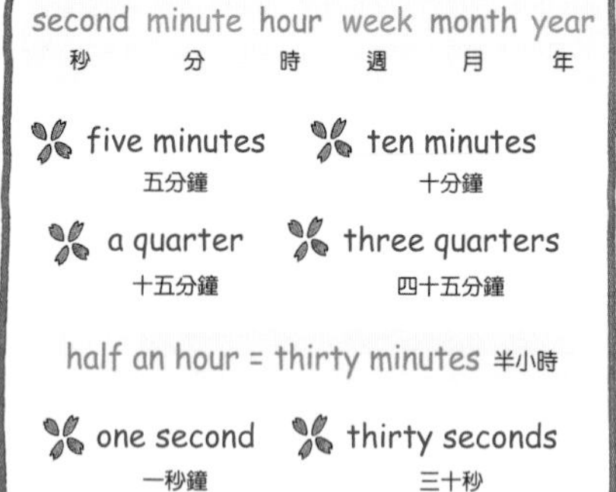

morning 早上

noon 中午

afternoon 下午

evening 傍晚

night 夜晚

midnight 午夜

Example

What time is it? 現在幾點？

It's nine-twenty. 現在九點二十分。

時間（Time）的說法

1. 以o'clock表示整點，以am（或a.m.）表示上午的整點，以pm（p.m.）表示午後的整點。

   - seven o'clock 七點
   - 9 am 上午九點
   - 11 pm 晚上11點

2. 以「時 ＋ 分」表達一般的時間。

   - nine forty-two 9點42分
   - three twenty 3點20分

3. half 及 quarter 的時間說法：

   - half past ten 10點半
   - a quarter after four 4點15分
   - a quarter to eight 7點45分

4. after、past 及 to 的用法：

   - twelve after five 5點12分
   - fifteen after two 2點15分
   - five past one 1點5分
   - eight to six 5點52分

What time is it, please? 請問現在幾點？
= What's the time, please?
It's seven forty-five. 7點45分。

表時間的介系詞

說明時間通常會使用固定的介系詞，請參考以下範例：

- in the morning
- in the afternoon
- in the evening
- at night
- at six o'clock
- at seven-thirty

4 Dates（○月○日）

January	February	March	April
一月	二月	三月	四月
May	June	July	August
五月	六月	七月	八月
September	October	November	December
九月	十月	十一月	十二月

first	second	third	fourth	fifth
1日	2日	3日	4日	5日

eleventh	sixteenth	twenty-second
11日	16日	22日

- February sixteenth 2月16日
- October fourth 10月4日
- August 29, 1996 1996年8月29日
- December 25, 2008 2008年12月25日

Example 1

When is your flight?
你搭幾號的飛機？

It's on November 18th.
11月18日。

When will you go back to Taiwan? 你什麼時候要回台灣呢？

August 10. 8月10號。

日期（Dates）的表達方式

1. 美式英語的日期寫法為0月0日00年，英式英語則是0日0月00年。

	2006年8月23日	2015年4月15日
美式英語 數字表示法	August 23, 2006 8-23-2006	April 15, 2015 4-15-2015
英式英語 數字表示法	23 August, 2006 23.8.2006	15 April, 2015 15.4.2015

2. 年代的說法如下：

年代	口語說法
1983	nineteen eighty-three
2000	two thousand
2007	two thousand and seven
1800	eighteen hundred
1906	nineteen o six

3. 說明特定日期的介系詞需用 on，但說明特定的年分介系詞要用 in。

- I was born on April 1, which is April Fool's Day.
  我的生日是4月1號，愚人節。

- My parents were married in 1996.
  我父母在1996年結婚。

Part 1 基本

5 Days, Weeks and Years（星期與其他時間）

MP3 5

Monday 星期一　Tuesday 星期二　Wednesday 星期三

Thursday 星期四　Friday 星期五　Saturday 星期六　Sunday 星期日

weekdays 工作日（星期一至五）

weekend 週末

- last week/month/year 上週／上個月／去年
- this week/month/year 本週／這個月／今年
- next week/month/year 下週／下個月／明年

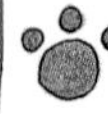

yesterday 昨天　today 今天　tomorrow 明天

the day before yesterday 前天

the day after tomorrow 後天

every day 每天

every week 每週

every month 每月

every year 每年

Example 1

Ⓐ What day is today? 今天星期幾？

Ⓑ Today is Sunday. 今天星期天。

Example 2

Ⓐ When did you arrive here in New York? 你什麼時候來到紐約的？

Ⓑ Last Saturday. 上星期六。

Dialogue 實用小對話

Receptionist:	Good afternoon, sir. How can I help you?
Guest:	I'd like to make a reservation for this Friday evening at 8:00.
Receptionist:	How many people will be in your party, sir?
Guest:	Five.
Receptionist:	Could you tell me your name and contact number, sir?
Guest:	Sure. My name is Jeffery Black. The phone number is 251-6184-333.
Receptionist:	Very good, Mr. Black. We're looking forward to seeing you and your party this Friday evening.
Guest:	Thank you very much.
Receptionist:	You are most welcome, Mr. Black.

櫃臺人員：午安！請問需要幫忙嗎？

顧客：我想要訂位，這個星期五晚上八點。

櫃臺人員：請問會有幾位貴賓呢，先生？

顧客：五位。

櫃臺人員：可以請您留下姓名與聯絡電話嗎，先生？

顧客：沒問題，我叫傑佛瑞．布雷克，電話號碼是251-6184-333。

櫃臺人員：好的，布雷克先生，我們很期待您與其他貴賓星期五晚間的光臨。

顧客：謝謝你。

櫃臺人員：不客氣，布雷克先生。

6 Time Periods（期間）

How long will it take? 這要花多久時間？

○小時

How many hours? 多少小時？
one hour 一小時
two hours 兩小時
five hours 五小時

○分

How long? 多久？
one minute 一分鐘
five minutes 五分鐘
twenty minutes 二十分鐘

○天

How many days? 多少天？
one day 一天
three days 三天
seven days 七天

○禮拜

How many weeks? 多少週？
one week 一週
two weeks 兩週
three weeks 三週

○個月

How many months? 多少個月？
one month 一個月
two months 兩個月
six months 六個月

○年

How many years? 多少年？
one year 一年
two years 兩年
three years 三年

Ⓐ How long will the application take?
申請程序要花多久時間？

Ⓑ It will take at least two weeks.
至少要花兩個星期。

1. 以 since 與 for 表達時間的差異

for 用於表示某狀況已持續多久的時間。since 是「自從」的意思，用於說明某事從某個時點開始，並一直持續維持。since引導的時間片語，句子常用完成式／完成進行式。since引導的子句用過去式時，主句用完成式／完成進行式。

1. We've been here for three days. 我們來到這兒已經三天了。
2. We've been here since Sunday morning.
我們從星期天早上起就來到這兒了。
3. I've been waiting here in the lobby for half an hour.
我已經在這大廳等了半小時了。
4. I've been waiting here since 9 am. 我從早上九點就一直在這裡等。
5. Mr. and Mrs. Richardson have been our Sky Ski Resort guests for four days. 李察森夫婦已經在我們天空滑雪度假中心待了四天。
6. Mr. and Mrs. Richardson have stayed at our Sky Ski Resort since last Friday.
李察森夫婦從上星期五就一直待在我們天空滑雪度假中心。

2. take 及 spend 的用法

1. take 及 spend 都有「花費時間」的意義，但是用法不同。
2. 以 take 表達花時間的句型
   - It takes + 人 + 時間 + 帶to的不定詞
   - 某事 + takes + 人 + 時間
   - 人 + take(s) + 時間 + 帶to的不定詞
3. 以 spend 表達花時間的句型
   - 人 + spend + 時間 + V-ing
   - 人 + spend + 時間 + on + 某事

1. It took Sarah two hours to get ready. 莎拉花了兩個小時才準備好。
2. Our journey to Europe will take 15 days.
我們到歐洲的行程要花十五天。
3. I spent three hours finishing the report. 我花了三小時完成這份報告。
4. Jason and I spent the whole weekend on the beach.
傑森跟我整個週末都待在海灘。

7 Greetings/Saying Goodbye （招呼語）

MP3 

Good morning. 早安！	Good afternoon. 午安！
Good evening. 晚安！	Good night. 晚安／再見！
Long time no see. 好久不見。	How are you?/ How do you do? 你好嗎？
Excuse me. 不好意思。（請別人幫忙的發語詞）	Thank you./ Thanks a lot. 謝謝。
You are welcome./ Don't mention it. 不客氣。	After you. 您先請。
Good-bye. 再見。	Good luck. 祝好運。
Take care. 保重。	I'm sorry. 抱歉，我不會說英語。 I don't speak English.
Would you please do me a favor? 可以請你幫個忙嗎？	

「抱歉」的兩種說法：

1. I'm sorry. 我很抱歉。 對他人表達歉意時的說法。
   例 I'm sorry to be late. 抱歉我遲到了。
2. Excuse me. 抱歉。 預先請求他人諒解的發語詞。
   例 Excuse me, I have to leave now. 抱歉，我得離開了。

Useful Expressions
打招呼與道再見的常見用法

How are you? 最近好嗎？
= How are you doing?
= How are things?
= How is everything?
= How's everything going?
= What's up?（較不正式的用法）

肯定回答

I'm fine. Thank you.
我很好，謝謝。

I'm great. 我很好。

Not so bad. 還不錯。

否定回答

I don't feel good.
我覺得不太舒服。

I feel awful. 我覺得很糟。

Long time no see. 好久不見。
= It's been a long time.

Nice to meet you. 很高興認識你。
= Glad to meet you.

Good-bye. 再見。
= Bye-bye.
= So long.
= See you.

I'll be seeing you. 再見。

I have to go now. 我得走了。

8 Introduction （介紹）

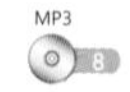

He/She is my . . . 他／她是我的……。

father/mother 爸爸；媽媽	uncle 叔；伯；舅
brother/sister 兄弟；姊妹	aunt 姑姑；嬸嬸
husband/wife 先生；太太	boyfriend/girlfriend 男朋友；女朋友
cousin 堂表親	best friend 好朋友

英文	中文	說明	用法
sir	先生	下對上的尊稱，或是書信中對男性的稱呼，通常不與姓名連用（在美國口語中 sir 不分性別）	Good morning, sir.
madam	女士；小姐	對婦女的尊稱，已婚、未婚皆適用	May I help you, madam?
Miss	小姐	對年輕女子或未婚女性的稱呼，置於姓名前	Miss White
Ms.	女士；小姐	對已婚或未婚的女性的稱呼，置於姓名前（在現代英語中常用來代替 Miss 和 Mrs.）	Ms. Black
Mr.	先生	Mister 的縮寫，用於男士的姓名或職務之前	Mr. Brown
Mrs.	夫人；太太	對已婚婦女的尊稱，通常與夫姓連用	Mrs. Green

Dialogue 實用對話

What should I call you? 我該怎麼稱呼你？

My name is Jack. 我叫傑克。

I'm from Taiwan. 我從台灣來。

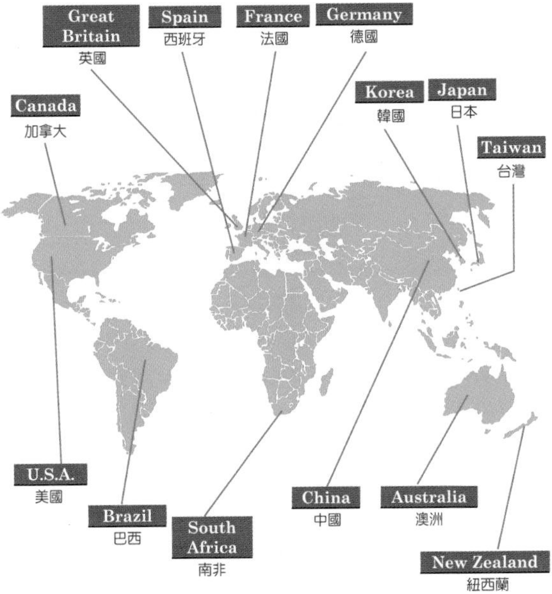

❾ Request and Help（請求幫助）

Could you please . . . ? 可以麻煩你……？	
Would you please write it down? 可以請你寫下來嗎？	Would you please speak more slowly? 可以請你說慢一點嗎？
Would you please say that again? 麻煩你再說一遍好嗎？	Wait a moment, please. 請稍等一下。
May I have your phone number? 可以告訴我你的電話號碼嗎？	Could you tell me the answer? 請你告訴我答案好嗎？
Could you give me a hand? 可以幫我一下嗎？	Help yourself. 自己來，別客氣。

Ⓐ How are you doing? 你好嗎？ Ⓑ I'm doing great. 我很好。	Ⓐ I have to go now. 我得走了。 Ⓑ See you later. 再見。
Ⓐ Thank you for your help. 謝謝你的幫忙。 Ⓑ No problem. 別客氣。	Ⓐ Can you give me your email address ? 可以告訴我你的電子郵件信箱嗎？ Ⓑ I beg your pardon. 不好意思，請再說一次。

Dialogue 實用對話

A: Where are you from, Ms. Keaton?
B: I'm sorry. I didn't quite hear what you said.
A: What country are you from?
B: Britain. London, actually.

A: 基頓小姐，請問妳是哪裡人？
B: 對不起，我沒聽清楚你剛剛說什麼。
A: 你是哪一國人？
B: 英國，事實上是從倫敦來的。

A: Excuse me. May I use your bathroom?
B: Sure. It's at the end of the hall.
A: Thank you very much.

A: 不好意思，能跟您借一下洗手間嗎？
B: 當然，就在走廊盡頭。
A: 謝謝。

A: Excuse me, do you mind if I open the window?
B: Of course not. Do as you like.

A: 對不起，你介意我打開窗戶嗎？
B: 當然不介意，請便。

A: Could you please help me? I'm looking for a post office.
B: Just walk two blocks down the street, take a left, and you'll see it on the right.
A: Thanks a lot.

A: 可以請你幫個忙嗎？我在找郵局。
B: 沿這條街走兩條街後左轉，就在你右手邊。
A: 非常感謝。

10 Weather and Seasons（天氣與季節）

The weather report says it will be . . . tomorrow.
氣象報告說明天會……。

It's . . . today. 今天……。

	hot 熱		warm 暖和
	cold 冷		sunny 晴朗
	cloudy 陰天		rainy 下雨
	windy 颳風		foggy 起霧
	snowy 下雪		

The sun is fierce. I need . . .
太陽太大了，我需要……。

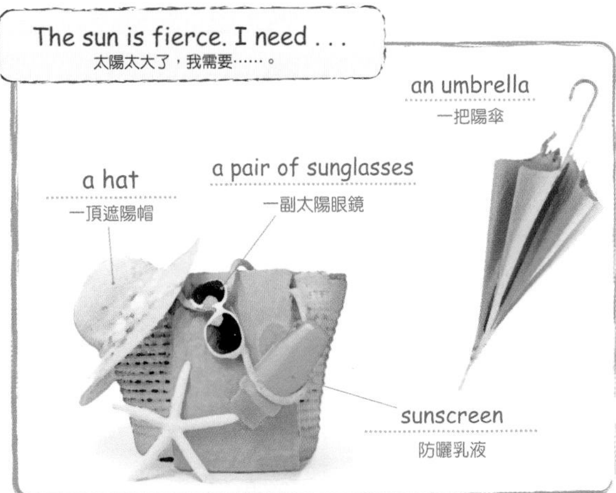

I suggest you bring . . . with you.
我建議你要帶……。

⑪ Inside the Airport 1 （機場內 1） MP3

	I-94 Form 美國出入境表格		check-in counter 報到櫃臺／驗票並領取登機卡
	fork and knife 刀叉		currency exchange desk 兌幣處
	chopsticks 筷子		duty-free shop 免稅商店
	wet napkin 濕紙巾		post office 郵局
	glass 杯子		public phone 公共電話
	newspaper 報紙		restroom 廁所
	pillow/blanket 枕頭／毛毯		bus/subway train 公車／地下鐵
	headset 耳機		smoking area 吸菸區
	duty-free brochure 免稅品手冊		priority seat 博愛座

Departure 出境程序

要出國的旅客，建議盡量在飛機起飛前兩個小時抵達機場，離境所需的文件包括：1. 護照 2. 機票 3. 出境登記表（針對外籍人士）

Step 1 → Check in 報到／登記

Step 2 → Baggage check in 檢查登記行李

Step 3 → Report to passport control 檢查護照

Step 4 → Security inspection 安全檢查

Step 5 → Board aircraft 登機

Arrival 入境程序

入境時需要準備的文件包括：

1. 護照 2. 海關申報書 3. 外籍人士另需 (1) 簽證 (2) 機票 (3) 入境登記表

Step 1 → Disembark from the aircraft 下飛機

Step 2 → Report to passport control 檢查護照

Step 3 → Retrieve your baggage 領回行李

Step 4 → Animal and plant inspection and quarantine 動植物防疫檢查

Step 5 → Baggage inspection 檢查行李

Supplementary Vocabulary 實用單字補充

international airport 國際機場	airline 航空公司	
Terminal 1/2 第一／二航廈	airfare 票價	customs 海關
departure tax 離境稅	transit 轉機	emergency exit 緊急出口
declare 申報	baggage claim check 行李提單	runway 跑道

 Inside the Airport 2 （機場內 2） MP3 

I want . . . ticket. 我要一張……機票。

	a single（英式） a one-way（美式） 單程		a return（英式） a round-trip（美式） 來回
	an economy-class 經濟艙		a business-class 商務艙
	a first-class 頭等艙 		a non-stop 直飛的

Would you prefer first class, business class or economy?
您要頭等艙、商務艙還是經濟艙？

When do you want to leave? 您要何時啟程？

Which flight do you want to take? 您要搭乘哪一個航班？

Where do you want to sit, window or aisle?
請問您想坐靠窗還是靠走道的位子？

An economy-class ticket is $500.
經濟艙的票是美金500元。

I'd like a return ticket from . . . to . . .
我要一張從……到……的來回票。

New York 紐約	London 倫敦
Los Angeles 洛杉磯	Edinburgh 愛丁堡
Miami 邁阿密	Cardiff 卡地夫（英國）
Las Vegas 拉斯維加斯	Belfast 貝爾法斯特（英國）

How much is a ticket to Miami? 到邁阿密的機票一張多少錢？

Is it a direct flight to Amsterdam?
這是直飛到阿姆斯特丹的班機嗎？

This is not a direct flight. You need to transfer in Bangkok.
這不是直飛的班機，您需要在曼谷轉機。

I would like to change my return flight to Los Angeles.
我想更改回程飛洛杉磯的班機。

13 Airports and Airlines （機場／航空公司）

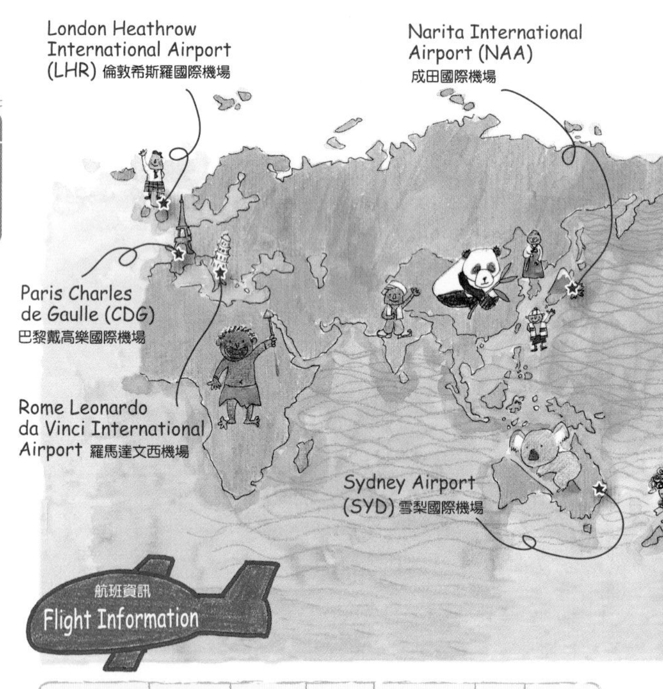

航班資訊
Flight Information

Schedule Date 預定日期	Schedule Time 預定時間	Airlines 航空公司	Flight No. 班機編號	Destination 目的地	Gate 登機門	Terminal 航廈
2015/08/09	10:15	China Airlines	CX 469	Hong Kong	B6	1

Airlines 航空公司

CI	China Airlines 中華航空
BR	Eva Airways 長榮航空
EG	Japan Asia Airways 日亞航空
CX	Cathay Pacific Airways 國泰航空
SQ	Singapore Airlines 新加坡航空
EL	Air Nippon 日空航空
UA	United Airlines 美國聯合航空
NW	Northwest Airlines 西北航空
CO	Continental Airlines 美國大陸航空
FE	Far East Air 遠東航空
TG	Transport Thai Airways 泰國航空
KL	KLM Royal Dutch Airlines 荷蘭皇家航空

14 Immigration Procedures （入境）

Passport and flight ticket, please.
請給我您的護照和機票。

Do you want a window seat or an aisle seat?
請問您的座位要靠窗戶或是靠走道？

Can I have an aisle seat?
我想劃走道邊的位置可以嗎？

Please inform us beforehand if there is a fragile item in your baggage.
如果行李中有易碎物品，請先告知我們。

I do have a fragile item. This one.
我是有易碎物品，就是這個。

What is it in this bag?
這個袋子裡面是什麼？

There are just a few bottles of pills in the bag.
袋子裡就只有幾個藥瓶。

Please open your suitcase. I need to have a look.
請將皮箱打開，我得檢查一下。

No problem. 沒問題。

Here is your boarding pass. Have a nice trip.
這是您的登機證。祝您旅途愉快！

Thank you very much. 謝謝。

Where do I go to check in for my China Airlines flight to Hong Kong?
請問搭華航的飛機去香港要到哪裡登記？

Over there. 在那裡。

Dialogue 實用對話

A:	Please show me your passport, boarding pass and disembarkation card, please.	請出示護照、登機證與入出境登記表。
B:	Here you are.	在這裡。
A:	What is the purpose of your visit?	您這次旅行的目的為何？
B:	To visit my friend.	拜訪朋友。
A:	How long are you going to stay here?	這次會在這裡待多久？
B:	For 6 days.	六天。
A:	Where are you going to stay?	這期間您會住在哪裡？
B:	I'll stay with a friend.	我會住在朋友家。
A:	Do you have your return ticket?	您有回程的機票嗎？
B:	Yes. Here it is.	是的，在這裡。
A:	Okay. Here is your passport. Have a nice stay!	沒問題，這是您的護照，祝您玩得愉快。

Useful Expressions 實用例句

1. May I have a look at your passport and visa?
   可以看一下你的護照和簽證嗎？
2. Where are you from? 請問你是哪一國人？
3. How long are you staying here? 你會在這裡待多久？
4. Are you here for vacation? 你是來這裡度假的嗎？
5. Have you got anything to declare? 你有什麼東西要申報嗎？
6. Please show me your declaration form. 請出示申報單。
7. Please fill out this form. 請填好這張表格。
8. I'll be here for three weeks. 我會在這裡待三個星期。
9. I'm here on business. 我是來出差的。
10. I have nothing to declare. 我沒有什麼要申報的。

15 During the Flight （機艙內）

MP3 

May I have some . . . ? 可以給我一點……嗎？			
	water 水		hamburger 漢堡
	green tea 綠茶		curry 咖哩
	coffee 咖啡		Japanese food 日本料理
	orange juice 柳橙汁		Chinese food 中華料理
	apple juice 蘋果汁		chicken 雞肉
	red/white wine 紅酒／白酒		beef 牛肉
	black tea 紅茶		pork 豬肉
	coke/soda/pop 可樂／汽水		fish 魚
	beer 啤酒		vegetarian food 素食

Part 3 機場、機內

Supplementary Vocabulary 飛行中常見用語

1. 醫藥疾病篇

fainting 暈眩	diarrhea 腹瀉	vomiting 嘔吐
bruise 擦傷	sprain 扭傷	headache 頭痛
stomachache 胃痛	choke 噎到	cramp 抽筋
antacid 胃乳片	ointment 藥膏（塗抹用）	aspirin 阿斯匹靈

2. 飲食娛樂篇

baby food 嬰兒食品 | child food 兒童餐 | low-sodium food 低鈉餐

seafood 海鮮 | snacks 點心 | pure vegetarian food 全素餐

non-alcoholic beverage 無酒精飲料 | alcoholic beverage 酒精性飲料

in-seat movies 個人電影 | duty-free shopping 購買免稅商品

postcard 明信片 | poker cards 撲克牌 | radio 收音機 | earphones 耳機

3. 實用單字篇

flight attendant 空服員 | pilot 機長 | copilot 副機長

life jacket 救生衣 | seat belt 安全帶 | aisle 走道

takeoff 起飛 | landing 降落 | parachute 降落傘 | non-stop 直飛

non-smoking section 禁菸區 | emergency exit 緊急出口

16 Traffic（交通）

MP3 15

A: Where are you going?/
Where to? 請問要去哪裡？

B: Please take me to ______.
請載我到______。

Places	Transport 交通工具	
New York 紐約 London 倫敦 San Francisco 舊金山 Paris 巴黎 Tokyo 東京	train car	火車車廂
	subway	地下鐵
Wild Animal Park 野生動物園	bus	公車
Sea World 海洋公園	taxi/cab	計程車
the Louvre Museum 羅浮宮 the Eiffel Tower 艾菲爾鐵塔	ship	船
the Statue of Liberty 自由女神像	airplane	飛機
Disney Land 迪士尼樂園	train	火車
the British Museum 大英博物館	tram	路面電車
the Natural History Museum 自然歷史博物館	rickshaw/ricksha	人力車

Part 4 交通

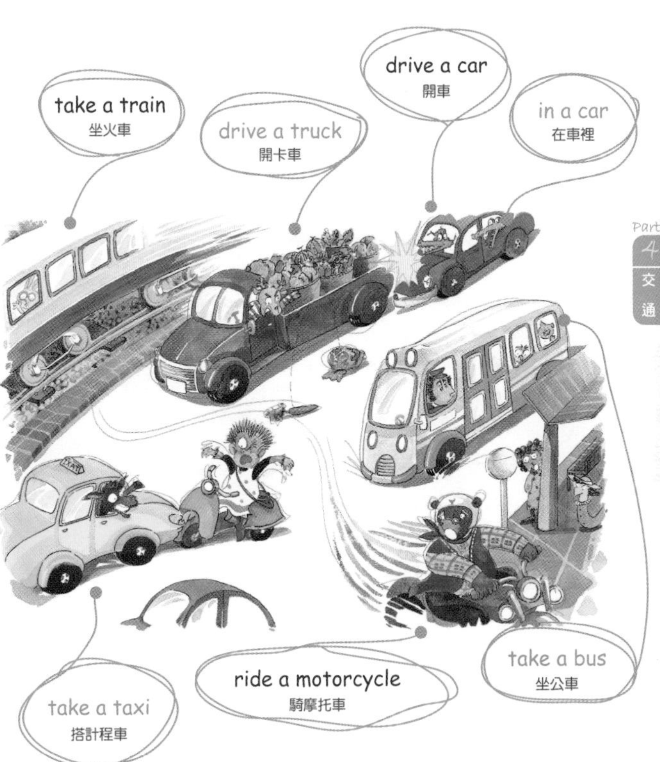
take a train
坐火車
drive a truck
開卡車
drive a car
開車
in a car
在車裡
take a taxi
搭計程車
ride a motorcycle
騎摩托車
take a bus
坐公車

Part 4 交通

17 Train Station 1（車站 1）

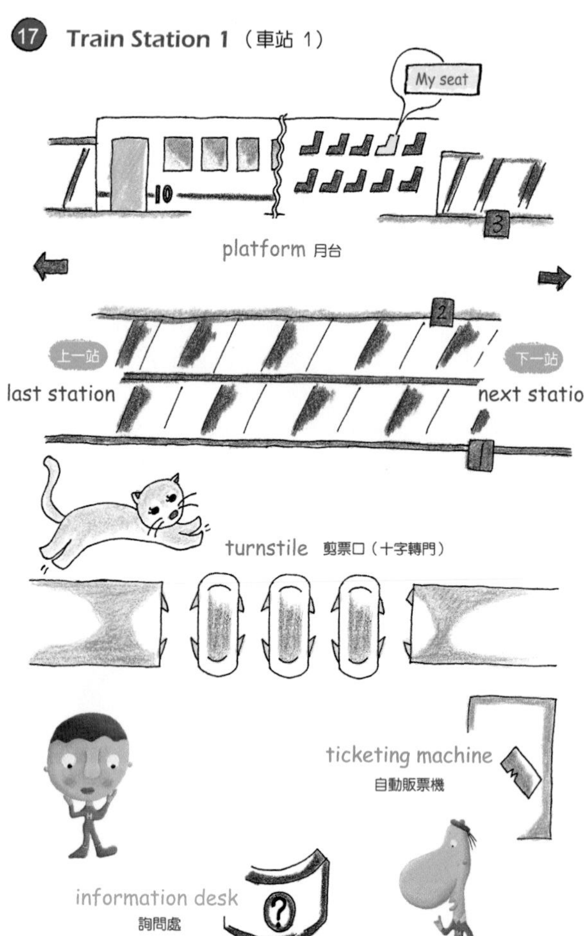

18 Train Station 2 （車站 2）

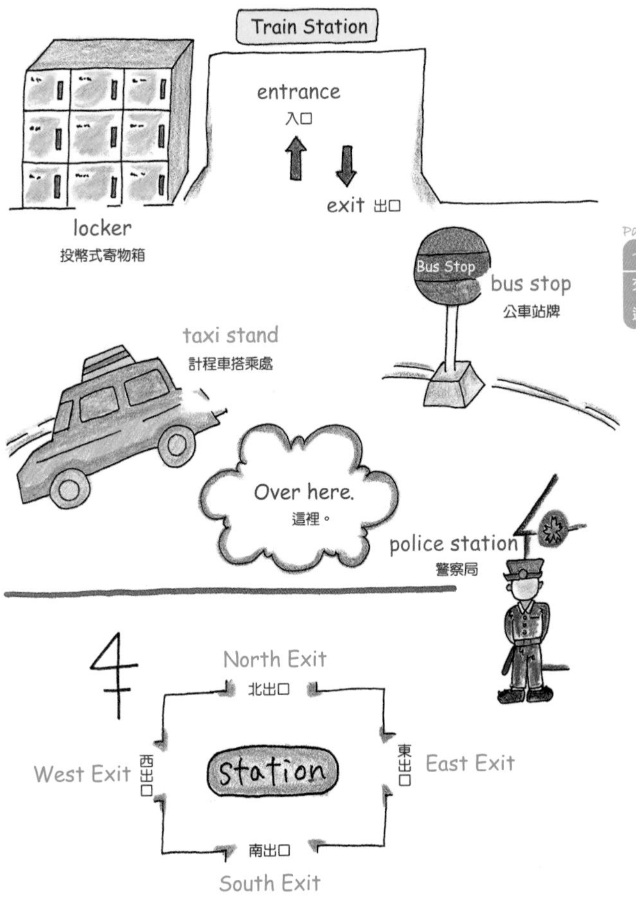

Part 4 交通

19 Buying Tickets（買車票） 

Three one-way tickets to New York, please.
三張到紐約的單程票，謝謝。

- ticket 車票
- circular journey ticket 周遊券
- one-week pass 一週券
- single journey ticket 單程票
- round-trip ticket 來回票
- sleeping berth 臥鋪
- dining car 餐車
- monorail 單軌鐵路或電車
- light rail 輕軌列車
- high speed rail 高速鐵路
- maglev train 磁浮列車
- seat reservation 預訂座位

1. Excuse me. Where is the nearest train station?
不好意思，請問最近的火車站在哪裡？
2. Where can I buy a ticket for the train?
請問我要去哪裡買火車票？
3. Which line should I take to go to the Ninth Station?
請問到第九火車站要搭哪一條線？
4. When is the next train to Tokyo?
下一班到東京的火車什麼時候會到？
5. Tickets for two adults to London, please.
兩張到倫敦的全票，謝謝。
6. I'll take an aisle seat. Thank you.
我要靠走道的位置。謝謝。

Part 4 交通

搭乘交通工具的說法

1. 說明搭乘的交通工具，可以使用「by ＋ 工具」。

- by car 坐車
- by bus 坐公車
- by train 坐火車
- by airplane 坐飛機
- by sea/ship 坐船
- by taxi 坐計程車

2. 說明位在交通工具中，則用不同的介系詞表示。

- in a car 在車裡
- on a bus 在公車上
- on a train 在火車上
- on a motorcycle 在摩托車上
- on a bicycle 在腳踏車上
- on a plane 在飛機上

3. 上下交通工具的說法如下：

- get in a car/get out of a car 上車／下車
- get on a bus/get off a bus 上公車／下公車
- get on a train/get off a train 上火車／下火車
- get on a ship/get off a ship 上船／下船

4. 駕駛交通工具的說法如下：

- drive a car 開車
- ride a motorcycle 騎摩托車
- drive a bus 駕駛公車
- drive a train 駕駛火車
- ride a bicycle 騎腳踏車

20 Taking the Train 1（搭乘火車或捷運 1）

one-day pass	one-day pass 一日券	upper / lower	upper/lower berth 上舖／下舖
	ticket stub 票根		traffic jam 塞車
Reserve Car 8 Seat 12	reserve a seat 劃位		route map 路線圖
	cancel a seat reservation 取消訂位		timetable 時刻表
	refund 退錢		nonsmoking seat 禁菸席
	adult 成人		smoking seat 吸菸席
	child 兒童		change trains 換火車
2	the second train car 第二節車廂		the first/last train 頭班車／末班車
3 12:00 YAMA	You should wait for the train to Edinburgh on Platform 3. 你要到愛丁堡應該到第三月台等車。		

各種大眾運輸系統名稱

Rapid transit 捷運	位於市中心的大眾運輸系統，以電力驅動，可行經地面、地下以及高於地面的軌道，是許多都會地區的重要運輸系統。
Subway 地下鐵	行經地面或地下的一種輕軌鐵道系統，美國許多大城市都以此為主要的大眾運輸工具。
Underground/ Metro 地下鐵	Underground 和 Metro 都是指地下鐵，和 Subway 的意義相似，都指行經地面下的鐵路運輸工具。在英國，通常以 Underground 表示倫敦的地鐵，Metro 反而是指市區以外的國家鐵路系統。
Elevated 高架鐵路	Elevated 是 Elevated railway 的縮寫，這種高架鐵路是指在市區道路上架起高臺的軌道上行駛的鐵路系統。
Tram 電車	在美國，電車往往指位在市區的觀光電纜車，外型類似公車，但行駛在軌道上，上方並有纜線牽引，行駛路線以停車場和遊樂區間為主。

票種

一般車票都會以距離及旅遊時間來區分，因此約有以下幾種票種：

One-way ticket 單程票	如果只到某地，之後不會再搭車，買單程票就是最划算的選擇。
Round-trip ticket 來回票	如果確定回程，建議在買票時就買來回票，通常比兩張單程票便宜，亦可省下再次買票的麻煩。
One-day pass 一日票	如果想在某地到處觀光，一天內會不斷出入地鐵站，購買此票種方便又划算。
One-week pass 一週票	如果待在某地時間較長，就可根據停留時間購買週票或是月票，有的會要求須附一張照片以貼在車票上。

TICKET
9:00 AM

21 Taking the Train 2（搭乘火車或捷運 2）

Is there a seat available on the train to Seattle?
到西雅圖的火車還有空位嗎？

Where do I change trains to go to Prague?
請問到布拉格要在哪裡轉車？

When is the next train to Toronto?
下一班到多倫多的火車幾點開？

How long does it take to Tokyo?
到東京要花多久時間？

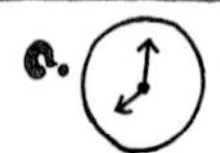

What line should I take to go to Vienna?
請問到維也納要搭哪一條線？

I didn't catch the train.
我沒趕上火車。

Where can I get a refund for these tickets?
我要到哪裡退這些票？

I have the wrong train.
Can you help me, please? 我搭錯車了，請問該怎麼辦？

Excuse me, please. I lost the ticket. What should I do now? 抱歉，我把票弄丟了，請問我現在該怎麼辦？

Useful Expressions 實用例句

May I please have a subway route map?
我可以拿一份地鐵的路線圖嗎？

Can I take this train to Atlanta?
去亞特蘭大是坐這班火車嗎？

Must I change trains? 我需要換車嗎？
= Do I have to change trains?

When does the train get in?
火車何時進站？

How much is the fare to Cape Town?
請問到開普敦的火車票價多少？

Where are the reserved seats?
請問預訂的座位在哪裡？

I took the wrong train. At which station should I get off?
我搭錯車了，要在哪一站下車才好呢？

At which station should I change trains?
請問我應該在哪一站轉車呢？

You needn't reserve seats on that train. It's never full.
搭那班火車不必訂位，它從不會坐滿。

A train just left about 5 minutes ago, and there's another one at 10:30. 有一班車5分鐘前剛開走，下一班是10:30開。

The next train leaves at 8 PM form Platform 2.
下一班車在晚上八點從第二月台開出。

You needn't change trains. It's a through train.
不必換車，這一班是直達車。

This is the right train. 搭這班車沒錯。

22 Taking the Bus/Taking a Taxi（搭乘公車／計程車）

MP3 19

 Catch a taxi. 攔計程車。 

To the Ritz Hotel, please. 麻煩到麗池酒店，謝謝。

Let me off here, please. 請讓我在這裡下車，謝謝。

How much do I owe you? 車資多少錢？

Thank you. Please keep the change. 謝謝，不用找錢了。

I have to get there by four. Would you hurry, please?
我得在四點以前到，可以請你開快一點嗎？

I'm sorry, but I'm in a hurry. 抱歉，我在趕時間。

Part 4 交通

 Take a bus.  搭公車。

I want to go to the local Sea World. Where should I get off?
我想到當地的海洋公園，請問我該在哪一站下車？

Please let me off at the next stop. 下一站下車，謝謝。

Please let me know when we are approaching the City Library.
快到市立圖書館時請告訴我。

How long will the bus be at this stop?
請問公車會在這裡停多久？

I think I just missed my stop. Can I please get off here?
我想我坐過站了，可以讓我在這兒下車嗎？

What time does the bus leave? 這班公車幾點開？

Supplementary Vocabulary 相關單字補充

city/local bus	市公車	tour bus	觀光巴士
articulated bus	連結公車	double-decker bus	雙層巴士
minibus	小型巴士	shuttle bus	接駁車
bus stop/booth	公車站	bus shelter	公車候車亭
taxi company	計程車公司	taxi rank/stand	計程車招呼站
fare	車資	tip	小費
customer service	客服	taximeter	計程車計費表
cabby/cabbie	計程車司機	on time	準時
drop … off	讓……下車	trunk	後車廂

Dialogue 實用對話

A: Where do you want to go? A: 請問要去哪裡？

B: I'm going to the airport. B: 我要到機場。

A: Get in. I'll take you. A: 上車吧，我載你去。

B: About how much will it cost? B: 大概要多少錢？

A: It will cost you 250 dollars. A: 250元。

B: On the meter? B: 依錶計費嗎？

A: No. A: 不是。

B: In that case, I think I'll try another taxi. B: 那我搭別台計程車好了。

Part 4 交通

 Renting a Car 1 （租車 1）

Do you have . . . ? 你們有……嗎？			
	a sedan 轎車		an SUV 休旅車
	a compact car 小車		a Ford Fiesta 福特的 Fiesta
	a BMW BMW 寶馬汽車		a Toyota Yaris 豐田的 Yaris

Useful Expressions 1 實用例句 1

1. Where can I rent a car? 我在哪裡可以租到車子呢？
2. What kind of cars do you have? 有哪幾種車款呢？
3. May I see your price and car list first?
   我可以先看有什麼價位和車款嗎？
4. When do I have to return the car? 最遲是什麼時候要還車？
5. Do I need to return the car with a full tank?
   還車時要加滿油嗎？
6. Is there an extra charge if I don't return it on time?
   車子如果沒有準時歸還，逾期的費用要怎麼算呢？
7. Does the price include insurance? 這個費用有含保險嗎？

Useful Expressions 2 實用例句 2

1. I would like it to have a satellite navigation system.
   我希望有衛星導航系統。
2. May I see the car before signing the contract?
   簽約前可以先看車嗎？
3. This car doesn't seem to be in very good condition. I'd like another. 這部車車況不佳，我想換別輛。

Dialogue 實用對話

A: How many days do you want to rent this car for?
這輛車你要租幾天？

B: Two days. What is the rate? 兩天。租金是多少？

A: It costs $50 per day. 一天是美金50元。

B: Is there mileage limit? 有行駛哩程數的限制嗎？

A: Yes, there is a mileage limit of 50 miles.
有的，有50英里的哩程限制。

B: Do I have to pay a deposit? 我需要付押金嗎？

A: You don't need to pay a deposit, but you have to leave some form of identification. 不需要押金，但是要押證件。

B: Can I return this car in Vancouver?
請問可以在溫哥華還車嗎？

A: You can return it at any of our branches.
您可以在我們任何一家分店還車。

24 Renting a Car 2 （租車 2）

I'd like to rent a car. 我想要租車。

May I see your international driving permit?
請出示您的國際駕照好嗎？

I want to return this car. Here is the rental agreement. 我要還車，這是租車契約書。

Hold on a second please. I need to check the car first. 請稍候，我要先檢查一下車子。

Could you please tell me about the scratch on the car? 車上怎麼會有刮痕？

I must have dented it when I opened the door. But it's not that bad.
一定是開車門時不小心撞凹的，可是並不明顯。

Could you please tell me about the dent on the car?
車上怎麼會有凹痕？

I didn't do it. It must have been there all along.
不是我弄的，應該是原本就有的。

▶ 國際駕照

若你打算到當地租車或買車駕駛，必須事先申請國際駕照。不過，有些國家不承認我國國際駕照，如日本、雪梨、荷蘭、越南等國。雖然這些國家可用我國國內駕照換發當地駕照，但大多手續複雜。而國內駕照若被吊銷，則國際駕照的效力也同時取消。

國際駕照的申請手續十分簡便，效期與國內駕照相同，申請當日即可取得。另外，國際駕照不同於一般駕照，它能將五種不同的駕駛車種登錄在同一本駕照上，所以申請者可同時持有小客車和機車的駕照在一本國際駕照上，申請費用相同。國際駕照有效期限最長三年，若在台灣的駕照有效期限低於三年，則依駕照的有效期限為準。

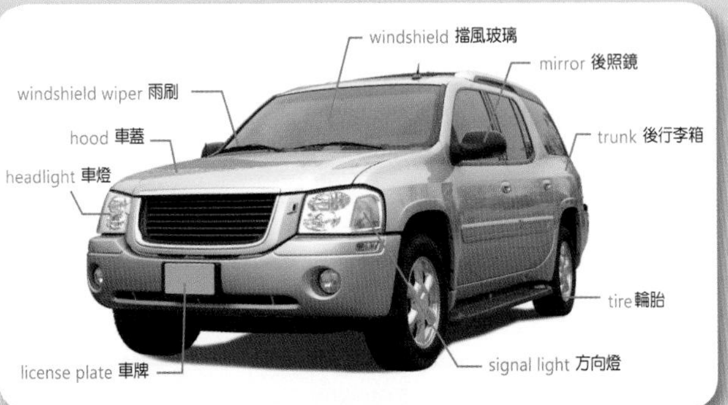

steering wheel 方向盤 emergency brake 手煞車 gauge 儀表板

horn 喇叭 gear 排檔桿 exhaust pipe 排氣管

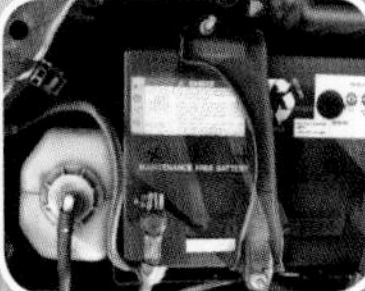

engine 引擎 battery 電瓶 jumper cables 救車線

25 Driving a Car （開車）

MP3 22

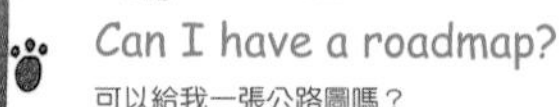

Can I have a roadmap?
可以給我一張公路圖嗎？

Where can I get on the freeway?
要怎麼上高速公路？

Can I park here for a while?
請問這裡可以臨時停車嗎？

Is there a parking lot around here?
請問這附近有停車場嗎？

What is the hourly rate for parking here?
停車費每小時多少錢？

We'll have to keep to the right.
我們必須靠右行駛。

補充單字

parking meter 停車計費表	parking lot 停車場	tire pressure 胎壓
parking space 停車位	crosswalk 行人穿越道	tollgate 收費站
fuel tank 油箱	flat tire 爆胎	rest area 休息站

26 Filling Up the Tank （加油） MP3 23

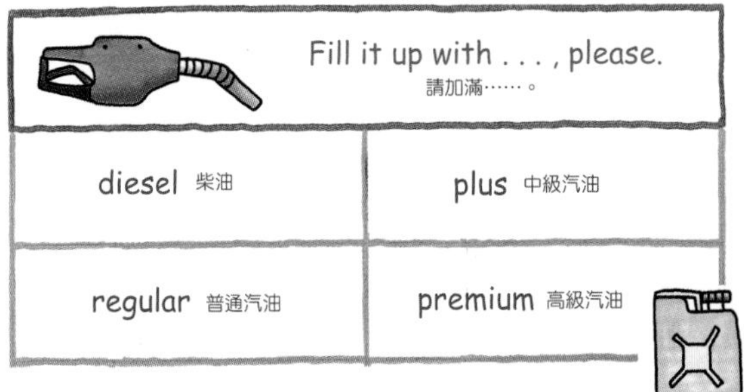

Fill it up with . . . , please. 請加滿……。	
diesel 柴油	plus 中級汽油
regular 普通汽油	premium 高級汽油

Useful Expressions 常用例句

1. Are there any gas stations nearby? 請問附近有加油站嗎？
2. What kind of gas do you want? 您要加哪一種汽油？
3. How much gas do you want? 要加多少汽油？
4. Give me 10 gallons of unleaded gas. 加10加侖的無鉛汽油。
5. 10 dollars of unleaded gas. 加10元的無鉛汽油。
6. How much for one gallon? 請問一加侖多少錢？
7. Can I pay with a credit card? 我可以刷卡嗎？
8. I'd like a car wash. 我要洗車。
9. Clean the windshield, please. 請幫我清潔擋風玻璃。
10. Fill it up with unleaded and check the oil, please.
    請加滿無鉛汽油，還有檢查一下機油。
11. Please check the tire pressure for me. 請幫我檢查一下胎壓。

 In a Hotel 1（飯店 1）

When should I check in/check out? 我該什麼時候登記住房／退房？	Which floor is it on? 在哪一層樓？
check in 登記住宿	hotel restaurants 飯店內餐廳
check out 退房	bar 酒吧
name/address 姓名／地址	swimming pool 游泳池
signature 簽名	gym 健身房
passport 護照	reception 接待櫃臺
breakfast coupon 早餐券	snack bar 點心販賣部
laundry service 洗衣服務	café/tea shop 咖啡廳／茶館
morning call 客房叫醒服務	laundromat 洗衣部
room service 客房服務	vending machine 自動販賣機

Dialogue 實用對話

A: Park Resort Hotel. How can I help you?
公園度假飯店，需要為您服務嗎？

B: Do you have a double room with a private shower?
請問有附個人衛浴的雙人房嗎？

A: Yes, but only on the top floor. 有，但是是在頂樓。

B: That's okay. How much does it cost? 那沒問題，多少錢？

A: It's 500 dollars a night. 一個晚上500元。

B: I'd like to book a double room with a private shower.
我要訂一間有個人衛浴的雙人房。

A: When for, Ms.? 小姐，請問要訂哪一天？

B: From September 2 for three days. 從9月2日起一共三天。

A: Just a moment, Ms. . . . There's no problem.
What's the name, and credit card number, please?
請稍等一下，……嗯，沒問題，請問您的姓名以及信用卡號？

B: Bonnie James. My VISA card number is 678 4434 25 54, and its expiration date is January 11th next year.
邦妮．詹姆斯，我的信用卡號碼是678 4434 2554，到期日是明年的1月11日。

A: Bonnie James, a double room with a private shower from September 2 for three days, and your VISA card number is 678 4434 2554.
好的，邦妮．詹姆斯小姐，您訂的是一間有衛浴的雙人房，從9月2日起共3天，您的信用卡號為678 4434 2554。

B: That's right. Thank you. 沒錯，謝謝！

A: Thank you very much for calling. 謝謝您的來電。

28 In a Hotel 2（飯店 2） MP3 25

Could you give me a new one, please? 可以給我一個新的嗎？		Can you recommend a restaurant near the hotel? 可以請你推薦在飯店附近的餐廳嗎？	
	quilt/pillow 被子／枕頭		spot 名勝
	blanket 毛毯		scenery 風景
	bed sheet 床單		diner 小餐館
	towel 毛巾		Japanese food 日本料理
	shampoo 洗髮精		bar 酒吧
	body shampoo 沐浴乳		Ramen 拉麵
	soap 肥皂		sushi bar 壽司吧
	bathrobe 浴袍		coffee house 咖啡屋
	room 房間		souvenir 紀念品

Part 5 飯店

Supplementary Vocabuary（飯店內的設施與服務）

restaurant 餐廳	swimming pool 泳池	childcare 幼兒照顧
conference room 會議室	broadband Internet 寬頻上網	
climate control 空調	minibar 房內的小冰箱	cable TV 有線電視
pay TV 付費電視	bedspread 床罩	closet 衣櫃
blinds 百葉窗	carpet 地毯	clothes hanger 衣架
ironing board 熨衣板	mat 踏腳墊	bathtub 浴缸
shower 淋浴	tile 磁磚	sink 洗手台
water pipe 水管	towel rack 毛巾架	drain 排水管
leak 漏水	shower cap 浴帽	dryer 吹風機
water heater 熱水器	electric razor 電鬍刀	toilet paper 衛生紙
faucet 水龍頭		

Useful Expressions 常用例句

1. Could you please give me two more towels?
請問可以再多給我兩條毛巾嗎？

2. Where can I get some hot water to drink?
請問哪裡有熱開水可以喝？

3. The hair dryer is not working. Can I have another one?
吹風機壞了，可以再拿一個給我嗎？

4. Please show me how to use the safe in my room.
請告訴我房裡的保險箱該怎麼用？

5. I left my key in the room. Could you open the door for me?
我把鑰匙忘在房裡了，請問你可以幫我開門嗎？

6. I need a morning call at 7:30 tomorrow.
明天早上7點半請打電話叫醒我。

7. How do I make an international call? 我該怎麼撥打國際電話？

29 Problems and Complaints（飯店內的糾紛）

The air conditioner is not working. 空調壞掉了。

	key 鑰匙		electric light 電燈
	air conditioner 空調		refrigerator 冰箱
	television/TV 電視		showerhead 蓮蓬頭
	telephone 電話		hair dryer 吹風機
	toilet 馬桶		electric kettle （保溫）水壺

The toilet is leaking.
馬桶在漏水。

The door lock is broken.
門鎖壞掉了。

boiled water 開水	tap water 自來水	key card 鑰匙卡	lock 鎖

We're out of toilet paper.
我們沒有衛生紙了。

The room we are in is too noisy.
我們的房間實在太吵了。

Useful Expressions 常用例句

1. The bellhop didn't bring up our baggage.
大廳服務生沒有幫我們把行李拿上來。

2. We need more toilet paper.
我們需要多一點衛生紙。

3. The toilet won't flush at all.
馬桶根本不能沖水。

4. The showerhead is clogged up.
蓮蓬頭塞住了。

5. We need some more clean towels.
我們還需要一些乾淨的毛巾。

6. I can't find an ashtray in the room.
我在房間裡找不到菸灰缸。

7. The housekeeper didn't clean the room. The carpet is filthy.
清潔人員沒有打掃房間，地毯髒得不得了。

8. The sheets need to be changed.
床單該換了。

9. Do you have a laundry service?
你們有衣服送洗服務嗎？

10. Can I use the Internet in the room?
我可以在房裡上網嗎？

11. I forgot my key card in the car. Could you open the door for me?
我把鑰匙卡忘在車上了，可以請你幫我開門嗎？

12. My plane is delayed three hours. Can I check out later?
我的飛機晚了三小時，我可以晚一點退房嗎？

 Service and Facilities（飯店內使用的單字） 

	bathroom 浴室		hot tub 熱水浴
	bed 床		public bathing 公共浴池
	map 地圖		hot spring 溫泉
	international telephone 國際電話		sauna 三溫暖／蒸氣浴
←0 10 50 card	telephone card 電話卡		men's room/ ladies' room 男廁／女廁
	plus tax 含稅	vacancy	vacancy 空房間
	emergency exit 緊急出口		a single bed 單人房
8 AM	breakfast 早餐	HOTEL	boutique hotel 精品旅館
12 PM	lunch 午餐		snack bar 點心吧
8 PM	dinner 晚餐		bed & breakfast (B&B) 含早餐的旅館（類似民宿）

飯店旅館比較

Hotel 飯店	hotel 便是一般我們所熟知的飯店，除了提供旅客餐飲住宿外，也發展出越來越多功能，為了吸引更多客源，許多飯店在觀光景點設立度假飯店，推出各種休閒設施。此外大多數飯店內都有大型會議室，結合商務功能，吸引公司企業前往飯店內開會。
Boutique Hotel 精品旅館	精品旅館和一般大型連鎖飯店不同，主要走精緻路線，傳達時尚、奢華的品味概念。旅館內通常沒有特殊的景觀或大型餐廳，只有小型點心吧提供顧客餐點飲食，房間內設備網路及有線電視，以商業人士為主要客戶。
Extended Stay Hotel 公寓式酒店	不同於一般大型飯店或小型旅館，讓旅客享受如同居住在家一般的服務，房間裡除了一般飯店房間擁有的衛浴設備外，也會有廚房、洗衣烘衣等一般家庭會用到的設施。
Motel 汽車旅館	汽車旅館與上述幾種飯店不同，提供個別房間與單獨的車位供旅客住宿，大部分汽車旅館為L型及U型建築，部分旅館內設有小型餐廳提供客人食物，而大多數汽車旅館都以顯眼的霓虹燈招牌吸引客人的注意。
B & B	B&B 指 bed 及 breakfast，是一種提供早餐的私人旅館，類似民宿。經營者通常為家庭，提供客人個別的房間與衛浴，隔天並提供早餐。許多 B&B 都是由家族經營，提供住家多餘的房間給顧客，因此往往房間數量不多，因此建議行前需先訂位。

31 Hotel Services （飯店內的服務）

How do I get to the hotel from the airport? 我該怎麼從機場到飯店？		Do you have a vacancy for tonight? 你們今晚還有空房嗎？
I booked a room when I was in Taiwan. 我在台灣時已經訂好房間了。		I'd like a double room for two days. 我想要訂一間雙人房，住兩晚。
I made a reservation on the phone last night. 我昨晚已經打電話訂房了。		How much is it per night? 住一晚價格是多少？
I booked a single room for four days. 我訂了一間單人房，住四天。		single room 單人房
Can I get a discount if I stay one week? 住一星期可以打折嗎？		double room 雙人房
What time is breakfast served? 早餐幾點開始？		studio room 小型套房
Do you take traveler's checks? 你們收旅行支票嗎？		twin room 有兩張單人床的雙人房
		child bed 兒童床

May I leave it here? I'll come back soon.
我可以把東西寄放在這裡嗎？我很快回來。

No problem. Please fill out this form.
沒問題，請填好這份表格。

Dialogue 實用對話

A: I'm ready to check out now. 我現在要退房。

B: Sure, may I have your name and room number?
好的，請問您的姓名和房間號碼？

A: Mike West in Room 716. 麥克・維斯特，716房。

B: One moment, please. Here is your bill.
That comes to US $520 even.
請稍等。這是您的帳單，一共是美金五百二十元。

A: May I check it? 我可以核對一下嗎？

B: By all means, go ahead. 當然，請。

A: Do you take credit card? 你們收信用卡嗎？

B: Yes, we do. 是的，我們收信用卡。

Part 5 飯店

Useful Expressions 例句補充

1. I'd like to stay another three nights.
Do you have a vacant room?
我想要再多住三天，你們還有房間嗎？

2. I'm afraid that I have to check out one day earlier because of a change in my schedule.
我得提早一天退房，因為我的行程改了。

3. Would it be possible for me to check out at 2 pm?
我可以在下午兩點退房嗎？

4. The bill comes to US $ 320.
您的帳單一共是320美元。

5. Is that everything?
這是所有的費用嗎？

6. There is a mistake in the bill.
帳單金額有點問題。

Shopping （商店）

Excuse me. Where is the nearest ______ ?
請問最近的 ______ 在哪裡？

drug store/pharmacy
藥局／藥房

bookstore
書局

beauty store
化妝品香水店

DVD and CD store 唱片行

department store
百貨公司

shoe store
鞋店

shopping mall
購物中心

stationery store
文具店

supermarket
超級市場

cinema
電影院

clothes store
服飾店

convenience store
便利商店

gift shop
禮品店

travel agency
旅行社

bank
銀行

Supplementary Vocabulary 實用單字補充

one dollar store	一元商店	general store	雜貨店		
hardware store	五金行	hobby store	特定商品店		
hypermarket	大賣場	pet store	寵物店		
surplus store	舊貨店	chain store	連鎖商店		
display case	展示櫃	catalog	目錄		
brand name	品牌	marked price	標價		
sales tax	購物稅	sales clerk	店員	fake	假的；仿冒

Useful Expressions 實用例句

1. Where is the nearest shopping mall?
請問最近的購物中心在哪裡？

2. Is there a supermarket around the hotel?
飯店附近有超級市場嗎？

3. Is there a flea market in this city?
這個城市裡有跳蚤市場嗎？

4. I'm looking for a store that sells second-hand designer clothes.
我在找賣設計師二手衣的商店。

5. Is that store open on Sundays?
請問那家店星期天有開嗎？

6. When will Mitsukoshi department store have a sale?
三越百貨公司什麼時候會打折？

33 Shopping for Clothes and Shoes（購買衣物基本會話）MP3 30

May I help you? 需要為您服務嗎？

Is there anything I can do for you?
您有任何需要我服務的地方嗎？

I'm just looking around. Thank you.
我只是隨便看看，謝謝。

Can you show me that one, please?
可以請你拿那件給我看嗎？

Can I try it on? 我可以試穿一下嗎？

Which one would you recommend? 你推薦哪一件？

Can I get a discount if I buy more?
如果我多買一點可以打折嗎？

May I see something a little less expensive?
我想看看價格再低一點的商品。

It doesn't fit. 這件不合身。

I'll take it. 我要買這個。

Dialogue 實用對話

A: Can I help you, madam?

B: Do you have this sweater in a larger size?

A: What size are you?

B: I usually wear a size 8 sweater.

A: I think a size 8 will be fine for you.

B: By the way, may I see the white one?

A: Oh, I'm sorry, but a size 8 in white is out of stock.

B: Can you place an order for me?

A: I think so. Please leave your name and phone number on this form, and I'll call you.

A: 請問需要幫忙嗎，女士？

B: 這件毛衣有大一點的尺寸嗎？

A: 請問您都穿幾號？

B: 我通常是穿8號。

A: 我想8號您應該是可以穿。

B: 請問我可以看一下白色的嗎？

A: 很抱歉，這個顏色的8號剛好缺貨。

B: 你可以幫我調貨嗎？

A: 應該可以，請您留下姓名和電話號碼在這張表格上，我會再通知您。

34 Shopping Mall （購物中心）

MP3 31

Where can I find ______ ?

請問 ______ 在哪裡？

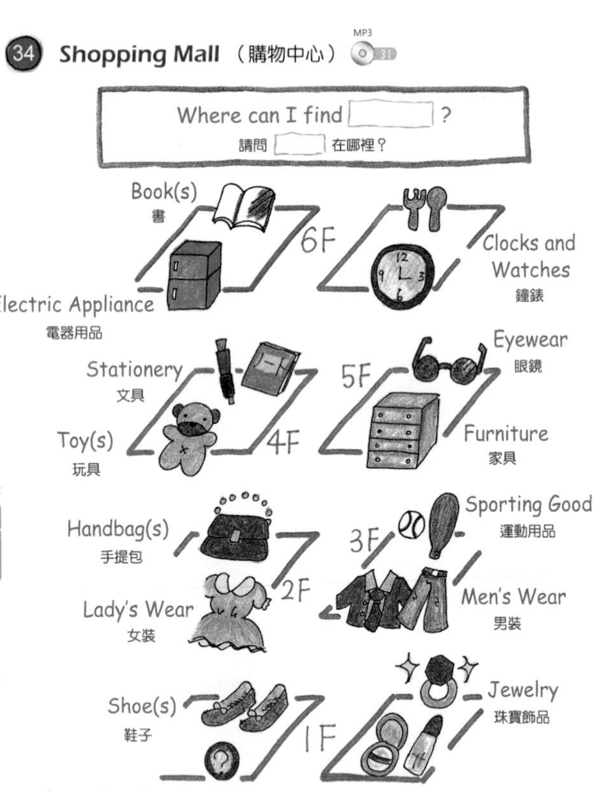

Part 6 購物

Main Street/ High Street	指主要的購物街道，通常位於大都市的繁華地區，整條街道各式商家林立，大多為零售商店。Main Street為美式用法，而High Street為英式用法。
Outlet Mall	折扣購物中心，屬於大型購物中心的一種，中心內的商店多由製造廠商直接經營，另外也販售過季商品，因此商品價格較其他購物中心比較起來更加划算。
Department Store	百貨公司，販售各式各樣的商品，商店都位於同一棟建築物內，依照商品的性質分配樓層，消費者可以在百貨公司內購買到各種產品。
Discount Department Store	折扣百貨商店，是一種大型的購物中心，店內也販售各式各樣有品牌的商品，價格比傳統商店更加優惠，部分折扣百貨商店著重販賣珠寶飾品和家電用品，美國最著名的折扣商店便是大型連鎖的Wal-Mart。
Anchor Store	主力商店，通常大型購物中心或百貨公司都會引進極受消費者歡迎的品牌，對該品牌廠商提供優惠的承租價格，進駐購物中心，藉由這些品牌商店對消費者的吸引力，相對提昇其他商品的消費。
Food Court	美食街，開放式的用餐區域，多位於購物中心或機場內。美食街當中有各種餐飲食物，消費者可自各開放櫃臺點餐，並在開放空間的位子上用餐。

35 Fitting 1（試穿 1）

Can I try it on? 我可以試穿嗎？

jacket 外套	underwear 內衣褲
shirt 襯衫	sweater 毛衣
t-shirt/T-shirt T恤	pants 褲子
coat 大衣	skirt 裙子
suit 套裝	jeans 牛仔褲

headwear 帽子；頭飾	helmet 頭盔
hat 帽子	stocking cap 針織帽
cap 帽（常為無邊而有帽舌）	

May I try on the shoes? 我可以試穿這雙鞋嗎？

pumps 無鞋帶有跟女鞋	sneakers 運動鞋
sandals 涼鞋	boots 靴子
high heels 高跟鞋	

Supplementary Vocabulary 單字補充

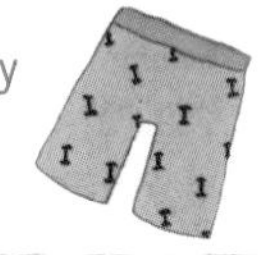

1. 衣著

blouse 女裝上衣	miniskirt 迷你裙	overall 連身衣褲
culottes 褲裙	slip 襯裙	jumper dress 連身裙
dress shirt 高領襯衫	suit jacket 西裝上衣	overcoat 外套大衣
cardigan 開襟毛衣	turtleneck 高領毛衣	pajamas 睡衣
V-neck V領衫	vest 背心	nightgown 女生的連身睡衣
bathing suit 泳衣	swimming trunks 泳褲	diving suit 潛水裝

2. 衣物材質

synthetic fabric 人造纖維	silk 絲	polyester 聚酯纖維
cotton 棉	leather 皮革	wool 羊毛
flax 亞麻布	down 羽絨	fur 毛皮

3. 衣著配件

belt 皮帶	button 扣子	buckle 扣環
zipper 拉鍊	tie 領帶	tie clip 領帶夾
collar 衣領	sleeve 袖子	pocket 口袋
lace 蕾絲；花邊	scarf 圍巾	Velcro 魔鬼粘

4. 鞋子種類

running shoes 運動鞋	sneakers 運動鞋	sandals 涼鞋
slippers 拖鞋	flats 平底鞋	flip-flops 夾腳涼鞋

36 Fitting 2（試穿 2）

MP3 33

Can I see the [ ] in the display case?
我可以看一下展示在櫃裡的 [ ] 嗎？

tie 領帶	clip earrings 夾式耳環
scarf 圍巾	pierced earrings 穿洞式耳環
shawl 披肩；圍巾	necklace 項鍊
belt 皮帶	bracelet 手鐲
ring 戒指	perfume 香水

Can you show me the [ ] in the window?
可以請你將櫥窗裡的 [ ] 拿給我看嗎？

glasses 眼鏡	sunglasses 太陽眼鏡

- Could you please measure the size for me?
  可以請你為我量尺寸嗎？
- Would you alter the jeans for me?
  可以請你幫我修改牛仔褲嗎？
- When will it be ready?
  什麼時候會改好？

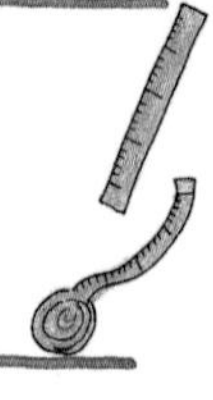

Part 6 購物

Supplementary Vocabulary 單字補充

jewelry 珠寶	gold 金	silver 銀
diamond 鑽石	coral 珊瑚	amber 琥珀
emerald 翡翠／綠寶石	pearl 珍珠	ruby 紅寶石
bead 珠珠	sequin 亮片	pendant 墜子
hair clip 髮夾	hair pin 髮簪	choker 短項鍊

Useful Expressions 常用例句

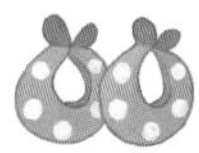

1. Would you please show me the platinum necklace?
可以讓我看看那條白金項鍊嗎？

2. Do you mind showing me the earrings in the display window? 可以麻煩你將櫥窗裡的耳環拿給我看一下嗎？

3. What size is this ring? 請問這個戒指是幾號的？

4. What brands do you carry? 你們這裡有哪些牌子？

5. I am looking for a waterproof watch.
我要買能防水的錶。

6. I would like a pair of sunglasses that block UVA and UVB.
我要買一副可以抗UVA和UVB的太陽眼鏡。

7. Do you have the latest mini perfume from Burberry?
你們有Burberry最新的迷你香水嗎？

8. What is your best seller during the holidays?
你們假期間什麼產品賣得最好？

Looking for Product Information（尋找商品）

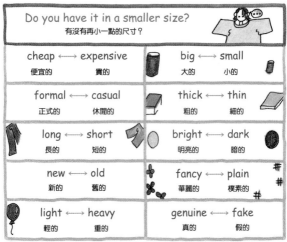

Do you have it in a smaller size?
有沒有再小一點的尺寸？

cheap ⟷ expensive 便宜的　貴的	big ⟷ small 大的　小的
formal ⟷ casual 正式的　休閒的	thick ⟷ thin 粗的　細的
long ⟷ short 長的　短的	bright ⟷ dark 明亮的　暗的
new ⟷ old 新的　舊的	fancy ⟷ plain 華麗的　樸素的
light ⟷ heavy 輕的　重的	genuine ⟷ fake 真的　假的

Do you have any other colors?
你們還有其他顏色嗎？
white
black
blue
red
green
purple
yellow
maroon
cerulean blue
gray
orange
pink

1. 在許多國家，購買商品的價格都含稅，包括美加、歐洲多數國家、亞洲的日本、泰國與新加坡等地。
2. 出國旅遊前往購物時，可以先查清楚每個國家的退稅標準。
3. 在多數國家中，消費金額若能達到一定的標準，便可以提出退稅，建議您在購買商品前，先詢問商家是否有退稅服務後再消費。

 Supplementary Vocabulary 單字補充

crimson 深紅	amber 琥珀色	aqua 碧綠色
beige 米色	brown 棕色	buff 米黃色
celadon 淡青色	cream 奶油色	cyan 藍青色
heliotrope 淺紫色	jade 翡翠綠	khaki 土黃色
navy blue 深藍色	peach 桃色	tan 褐色

 Dialogue 實用對話

A: Hi. I'm Amy Lee, and I'm a tourist from Taiwan. I just bought a pair of boots for $150. Can I get a tax refund?
你好，我是艾美．李，來自台灣的旅客。我剛剛買了一雙美金150元的靴子，請問可以退稅嗎？

B: I think so. May I see your passport, please?
我想是可以的。麻煩您出示護照好嗎？

A: Sure. Here you go. 好的，護照在這。

B: Thanks, Ms. Lee. I will give you a tax refund form. When you leave the country, take this form and the boots you bought to the customs desk at the airport. After confirming your information, they will stamp the form. Then mail it back to our office.
李小姐，謝謝，我會給您一張退稅單。您出境時，只要拿著這張單子和您剛買的靴子，到機場的海關櫃臺就可以了。海關會在確認您的資料後，在單子上蓋章，您只要把單子寄回本店就可以了。

A: Is that all? 這樣就好了？

B: Yes. After we receive the form, we will send you the refund check. 是的，我們收到單子以後，會寄退稅支票給您。

A: That's great. Thank you very much! 太好了，非常謝謝你。

38 Shopping for Cosmetics（化妝品）

Can I try on the foundation? 我可以試搽一下粉底嗎？	What is your skin type? 你是屬於哪一種膚質？
foundation 粉底	dry skin 乾燥肌膚
eyebrow pencil 眉筆	oily skin 油性肌膚
eye shadow 眼影	skin whitening 美白
liquid eyeliner 眼線液	anti-aging skin care 抗老
mascara 睫毛膏	acne treatment 治痘
lipstick/lip gloss 口紅／唇蜜	UV protection/sunscreen 抗UV／防曬霜
blusher 腮紅	lip balm/hand cream 護唇膏／護手霜
compact foundation 粉餅	lotion/moisturizer 化妝水／保濕霜
nail polish 指甲油	makeup remover 卸妝產品

Supplementary Vocabulary 單字補充

makeover 美容	manicure 手部護理（特別指修手指甲）	
pedicure 足部護理	nail clipper 指甲刀	nail file 指甲銼刀
shampoo 洗髮精	perm 燙髮	dye 染髮
hair gel/styling gel 髮膠	body lotion 身體乳液	deodorant 止汗劑
concealer 遮瑕膏	loose powder 蜜粉	pressed powder 蜜粉餅
eyelash curler 睫毛夾	powder puff 粉撲	facial mask 面膜

Useful Expressions 常用例句

1. What kind of special offers do you have on cosmetics right now? 你們的化妝品目前有什麼特惠嗎？
2. Do you have this lipstick in another color?
請問這種口紅還有別的顏色嗎？
3. I'm looking for waterproof mascara. 我要買防水睫毛膏。
4. Is there anything that will help cover this blemish on my face? 有什麼產品能遮住我臉上的這塊斑嗎？
5. I have sensitive skin and cannot use products that contain fragrance. 我的皮膚很敏感，不能用含香味的產品。
6. How often should I apply the lotion?
我應該多久搽一次乳液？
7. How does this product work?
這樣產品有什麼功能？
8. Where can I buy a roll-on deodorant?
請問到哪裡能買到滾珠式的體香劑？

Convenience Store（便利商店）

Have you got any disposable contact lenses?

請問你們有賣拋棄式隱形眼鏡嗎？

pen/pencil	筆／鉛筆	cleaning solution	隱形眼鏡清潔液
notebook	筆記本	facial cleanser	洗面乳
postcard	明信片	shampoo	洗髮精
toothbrush	牙刷	shower shampoo	沐浴乳
toothpaste	牙膏	socks	短襪
nail clipper	指甲剪	underwear	內衣
tissue	面紙	newspaper	報紙
razor	刮鬍刀	map	地圖
shaving cream	刮鬍膏	tampon/ sanitary napkin	衛生條／衛生棉

Supplementary Vocabulary 單字補充

calculator	計算機		envelop	信封	
paperclip	迴紋針		laundry detergent	洗衣粉	
hair conditioner	潤髮乳		beauty soap	洗面皂	
vitamin 維他命		dental floss 牙線		mouthwash 漱口水	
eye drops 眼藥水		Vaseline 凡士林		cotton swab 棉花球	

Dialogue 實用對話

A: Good afternoon, I would like some cigarettes, please.
午安，我要買菸，謝謝。

B: What kind would you like? 請問你要哪個牌子？

A: Which brand is cheapest? 哪個牌子的菸最便宜？

B: Try these. They're not very expensive. 試試看這個吧，不太貴。

A: All right, I'll take those. And I'd like a lighter, please.
好，就買這個。麻煩再給我一個打火機。

Useful Expressions 常用例句（詢問價格）

1. How much is this piece of organic soap? 這塊有機肥皂價格多少？
2. What about the price? 價格是多少？
=What's it worth? =How much do you want for it?
=How much do you say it is?
=How much do I owe you?
3. How much are these things altogether? 這些一共多少錢？
4. I would call it rather expensive. 這太貴了。
=The price is too high.
5. The price is not reasonable. 這價錢不合理。
6. Can you make it any cheaper? 可以再便宜一點嗎？

40 Electrical Appliance（電器用品）

Where is a good place to shop for electric goods?
哪裡是購買電器的好地方？

TV/LCD TV 電視／液晶電視	 digital camera 數位相機
 cellular phone/ cellphone 手機	 digital video recorder 數位錄影機
 fax machine 傳真機	 memory card 記憶卡
 MP3 player MP3 隨身聽	 battery 電池
 DVD player DVD 播放機	 electronic dictionary 電子辭典

desktop computer/laptop computer
桌上型電腦／筆記型電腦

wall clock/wristwatch/alarm clock
掛鐘／手錶／鬧鐘

What is the pixel rating of this camera?
這台相機的畫素是多少？

Does this camera focus automatically?
這台相機是自動對焦的嗎？

How many pictures can I take with a 1G card?
如果我用容量1G的記憶卡可以拍幾張照片？

Size D battery	Size C battery	Size AA battery	Size AAA battery
一號電池	二號電池	三號電池	四號電池

warranty 保證書 

manual 說明書 

Supplementary Vocabulary 單字補充

1. 電腦

application 應用程式	back up 備份	CPU 中央處理器
directory 目錄	DVD DVD	icon 圖示
keyboard 鍵盤	memory 記憶體	reboot 重新開機
scan 掃瞄	software 軟體	virus 病毒
ink-jet printer 噴墨式印表機		toner 碳粉匣

2. 數位相機

flash memory 快閃記憶體	resolution 解析度	
flash 閃光燈	battery capacity 電池壽命	
tripod 腳架	telescopic lens 伸縮鏡頭	diaphragm 光圈
interchangeable lenses 可更換式鏡頭	shutter 快門	

Useful Expressions 實用例句

1. What functions does this model have?
   這款相機有什麼功能？
2. What is this button used for?
   這個按鈕的功能是什麼？
3. What is the size of the memory stick?
   這記憶卡的容量是多少？
4. Can the lens take wide-angle shots?
   有廣角功能嗎？
5. I would like to have this film developed, please.
   麻煩你，我要沖洗這捲底片。
6. Please enlarge these photos to 5 by 7.
   請將這些照片放大到5 x 7。

41 Payment（付帳）

MP3 38

How much does it cost? = What's the price of this?
請問這多少錢？

It's a bit too expensive.
價錢有些貴。

Could you cut the price a little, please?
可以算便宜一點嗎？

30% off (thirty percent off)
價格減少三成，亦即打七折。

紅字部分可替換適當的數字。
英語打折的說法與台灣不同，數字中提到的是減去價錢的比例。

A: How would you like to pay, by credit card or cash?
請問您要用信用卡或現金付款？

B: I'll pay by credit card.
我要用信用卡付款。

A: Here is your change. 這是找給您的錢。

B: I think you gave me the wrong change.
我想你找錯錢了。

A: I'm sorry, sir. May I see your bill, please?
真抱歉，先生。我可以看一下您的帳單嗎？

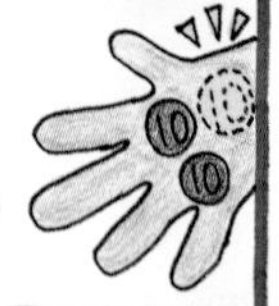

Thank you for visiting the Pacific Sogo Department Store. 感謝您光臨太平洋崇光百貨。

Dialogue 實用對話

A: Excuse me.
Can I have a look at this optical mouse?
對不起，我可以看一下這個光學滑鼠嗎？

B: Sure. Here it is. 當然可以，請。

A: How much is it? 這個多少錢？

B: NT $1,200. 台幣1,200元。

A: I'm afraid it's a bit too expensive.
Do you have something less expensive?
太貴了一點，你們有賣便宜一點的嗎？

B: Yes. That one costs NT $690.
有，那個只要690元。

A: I'll take that one, then. Thank you.
那我就買那個吧，謝謝。

Useful Expressions 實用例句

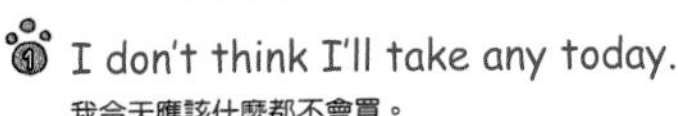

1. I don't think I'll take any today.
我今天應該什麼都不會買。

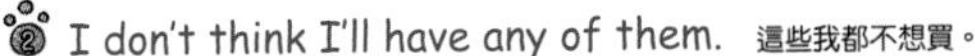

2. I don't think I'll have any of them. 這些我都不想買。
3. It's the thing for me. 這正是我想要的。
4. How much do you sell it for? 這多少錢？
5. I'll take this one. How much discount do you give?
我就買這個。你們打幾折？
6. Do you take traveler's check? 你們收旅行支票嗎？

42 Eating and Drinking 1（用餐基本會話 1）

MP3 

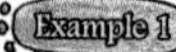

Example 1

Waiter: Good evening. Do you have a reservation?
晚安，請問你們有訂位嗎？

Guest: Yes. The name is Kimberly Johnson.
I reserved a table for three at 8pm.
有，訂位的名字是金柏莉．強生，我訂了八點鐘三個人的位子。

Example 2

Waitress: Would you care for a table in a smoking or a nonsmoking area?
請問您要坐在吸菸區或非吸菸區？

Guest: In a nonsmoking area, please. 非吸菸區，謝謝。

Smoking area 吸菸區

Nonsmoking area 非吸菸區

Example 3

Waiter: I'm sorry. We are fully booked. If you can wait in the bar for fifteen minutes, I will find a table for you. 抱歉，我們所有的位子都訂滿了。如果您願意在酒吧稍等十五分鐘，我可以幫您找到位子。

Guest: Thank you. That's very nice of you.
謝謝，你人真好。

Waiter: You're welcome. 不客氣。

OK!

Can I look at the menu, please? 我可以看一下菜單嗎？

What would you suggest?
你有什麼好推薦嗎？

What meal selections do you have? 你們有什麼餐點可以選擇？

food

drink

Example 4

Would you like me to serve the coffee at the same time?
您的咖啡要和主餐一起上嗎？

Yes, please. 好的，謝謝。

Useful Expressions 常用例句

1. I'd like to make a reservation for tonight.
我要訂今天晚餐的位子。

2. What are your dinner hours? 你們供應晚餐的時間是？

3. Do you have a minimum charge?
你們有最低消費嗎？

4. Do you have vegetarian dishes?
你們有素食餐點嗎？

5. What's today's special?
今日特餐是什麼？

Dialogue 實用對話

Waitress: Good evening, sir.
Guest: Good evening.
Waitress: Here is your menu.
Guest: Thank you.
Waitress: May I take your order now?
Guest: Could you give us a few minutes? We haven't decided yet.
Waitress: Sure, please take your time. I'll come back when you are ready.
Guest: Ah, thank you.

服務生：晚安，先生。
顧　客：晚安。
服務生：這是您的菜單。
顧　客：謝謝。
服務生：請問您現在要點餐了嗎？
顧　客：可以再給我們幾分鐘考慮嗎？我們還沒決定。
服務生：當然，請慢慢看。等您們準備好要點餐我再過來。
顧　客：謝謝。

43 Eating and Drinking 2（用餐基本會話 2）

MP3 

I'm starving to death!
我餓得不得了！

The bread was tasty.
Can I have another one?
這個麵包很好吃，可以再給我一份嗎？

I'm stuffed. 我好飽。

We've been sitting here for twenty minutes, and no one has come to serve the table.
我們已經坐下來二十分鐘了，但是一直沒有人來為我們服務。

It's too noisy here. Could you move me to another table?
這裡實在太吵了，可以請你幫我們換到另一桌嗎？

Can I get the check, please? 麻煩結帳。

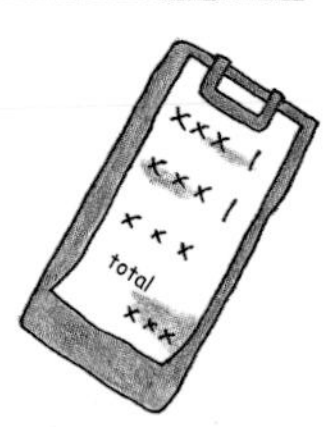

It's on me. 我請客。

Can we split the bill? 我們可以分開結帳嗎？

Thank you for inviting me to dinner.
謝謝你邀請我吃飯。

Can you give me a receipt, please?
可以開收據給我嗎？

Thank you. Have a nice evening.
謝謝，祝您有個美好的夜晚。

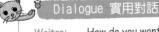

Dialogue 實用對話

Waiter: How do you want your steak? Medium or well-done?
您的牛排要幾分熟？五分熟還是全熟？

Guest 1: Medium, please. 五分熟，謝謝。

Guest 2: The same for me. 我也一樣。

Useful Expressions 常用例句

Excuse me. I ordered a roast beef sandwich forty minutes ago. Is it ready yet?
不好意思，我四十分鐘前點了烤牛肉三明治，請問好了嗎？

Could you give me a glass of lemonade?
麻煩你給我一杯檸檬水好嗎？

I don't think this pork rib is fresh.
我覺得這豬肋排不太新鮮。

Excuse me. I think you have made a mistake with my order. I didn't order lobster. 不好意思，你好像上錯菜了！我並沒有點龍蝦。

I'd like to cancel my order. 我要取消我點的餐。

I'm sorry. The kitchen is very busy today.
很抱歉，今天廚房實在很忙。

Your meal is on the house. Please accept our apology.
您的餐點免費，請接受我們的道歉。

Your lamb chop will come right away. 您點的羊排馬上就來。

If you don't like the taste of the fish, perhaps I could get you something else? 假如不喜歡這道魚的口味，要不要我為您換些別的？

I'll make sure the same mistake won't happen again.
我保證不會再發生同樣的問題。

 44 Tableware （餐具）  MP3 41

Can I have a fork and knife please?
可以給我一副刀叉嗎？

	chopstick(s) 筷子		fork 叉子
	spoon 湯匙		knife 刀子
	plate 盤子		drinking glass 杯子
	paper towel 紙巾		toothpick 牙籤

 Smoking bans 國外的禁菸狀況

多數歐美國家都禁止販售香菸給未成年的青少年。而在公共場合，以英美為例，幾乎全面禁止在室內的公開場合吸煙，包括餐廳、酒吧等，美國許多州更全面在公共場所禁煙，而許多餐飲服務業者則是會在室外區域設置吸煙區 (smoking section)。

Supplementary Vocabulary 單字補充

tableware 餐具	napkin 餐巾	serving tray 托盤
salad fork 沙拉叉	dinner knife 餐刀	dinner fork 餐叉
soup spoon 湯匙	butter knife 奶油刀	fish knife 魚刀
dessert spoon 點心匙	dessert fork 點心叉	serving spoon 公匙
serving fork 公叉	salt shaker 鹽罐	pepper shaker 胡椒罐
sugar bowl 糖罐	creamer 鮮奶油罐	sauce boat 船型醬料盅

餐桌禮儀

所謂餐桌禮儀（table manners）是指用餐時需遵守的禮節以及正確使用餐具的方法，各地的餐桌禮儀受不同文化所影響，當然也會依照實際情況不斷做調整。以下幾個國家便各有不同的餐桌禮儀：

英式餐桌禮儀	1. 用餐時需細嚼慢嚥，口中有食物時不應開口說話。 2. 手肘不能放在桌上。 3. 坐在餐桌前應盡量避免咳嗽或打噴嚏，若忍不住應先行離席。 4. 不能用手直接拿食物吃，除非是吃麵包時。
美式餐桌禮儀	1. 一道菜呈到桌上時應順序取至個人的盤中，拿完後再傳給下一個人。 2. 不要在盤子裡混合或攪拌食物。 3. 口中有食物時避免開口說話，談話也不要過於大聲。 4. 喝湯時盡量不要發出聲音，喝茶或咖啡時也應倒進杯子裡小口啜飲。 5. 盡量將面前所有的食物吃完。
日本餐桌禮儀	1. 日本人習慣大家一起坐在桌前吃飯，等所有人坐定並說「開動」後才可開動。 2. 吃麵的時候一定要發出聲音，並且越大聲越好，表示麵食很美味。 3. 以清酒佐飯時，若想要再喝，必須先將自己杯中的酒喝完才能再倒，若不想要再多喝，則讓酒杯保持倒滿的狀態。

45 Food Flavors（味道）

How do you like the pizza?
您覺得披薩的味道如何？

This pizza has a very special flavor. 這披薩的味道很特別。

I like it. 我喜歡。
I don't like it. 我不喜歡。

sweet 甜的
spicy 辣的
sour 酸的
salty 鹹的
bitter 苦的

plain 清淡的
heavy 口味重的
greasy 油膩的
light food/heavy food 清淡／口味重的食物
health food 健康食品

Dialogue 實用對話

Guest: Excuse me. I don't think the pork is properly cooked. It's still raw.

Waiter: I'm really sorry about that. I'll tell the kitchen to prepare a new one for you.

Guest: Also, I think you forgot my chicken salad. Could you check if it's ready?

Waiter: Sure. I'll be right back. I'm terribly sorry. I'll try to make sure the same mistake won't happen again.

顧　客：不好意思，我覺得豬肉沒有煮熟，這還是生的。
服務生：噢，很抱歉。我會叫廚房為您再做一份新的。
顧　客：還有，你好像忘了我有點雞肉沙拉，可以幫我看看做好了嗎？
服務生：好的，我馬上回來。非常抱歉，我保證不會再發生同樣的問題了。

Useful Expressions 實用例句

1. The food is off. 這道菜變質了。
2. The food has a funny taste. 這道菜的味道嚐起來很怪。
3. The food has no taste. 這道菜沒有味道。
4. The food is still cold. 這道菜還是冷的。
5. The food is overcooked. 這道菜煮得太熟了。
6. This is not the right flavor. 這個不是我要的口味。

46 Fast Food（速食）

Is it for here or to go?

請問您是內用還是外帶？

To go. 外帶。

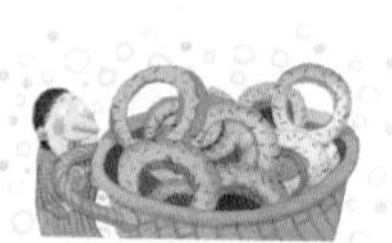

- hamburger 漢堡
- cheeseburger 吉士漢堡
- double cheeseburger 雙層吉士漢堡
- fishburger 魚堡
- riceburger 米漢堡
- sandwich 三明治
- pizza 披薩
- salad 沙拉

fried chicken
炸雞
french fries
薯條
chicken nugget(s)
雞塊
pancake(s)
美式鬆餅
ketchup 番茄醬
mayonnaise 美乃滋
ice cream 冰淇淋
milk shake 奶昔

Combo No. 2, please.

二號餐，謝謝。

combo，指套餐，可省略，直接說「No. 2, please.」也可以。

Useful Expressions 常用例句

1. I'd like two Mcchickens and one medium French fries to go. 我要兩個麥香雞和一份中薯外帶。
2. Can I replace the fries with onion rings? 我可以把薯條換成洋蔥圈嗎？
3. No pickles in my cheeseburger, please. 我的吉士漢堡裡不要加醃黃瓜。
4. It's faster to order at the drive through window than inside the restaurant. 在得來速窗口點餐比在餐廳裡面點要快。
5. Is your family size meal big enough for three adults? 你們的全家餐夠三個大人吃嗎？
6. Would you like to upgrade your meal to the large size? 您的套餐要升等為大分量的餐嗎？
7. It will take five minutes for the French fries to be ready. 薯條要等五分鐘。
8. What would you like with your hamburger? Ketchup? Mustard? 請問您的漢堡要配什麼？番茄醬還是芥末？
9. Please help yourself with the drinks. 飲料請自取。
10. You can have your own combination for the happy meal. 您可以自己組合快樂餐的內容。

Dialogue 實用對話

Good afternoon. What can I get you? 午安，需要什麼嗎？

Good afternoon. I'll have one large fries and two small black coffees. 午安，我要一份大薯和兩個小杯黑咖啡。

OK. One large fries and two small black coffees. Can I get you anything else?
好的，一份大薯和兩個小杯黑咖啡，還需要別的嗎？

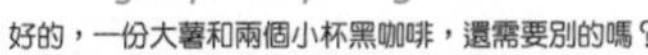

No. That'll be all. 不用，這樣就好了。

That's $4.99 in total. Please drive to the window now.
一共是4.99元，請把車開到窗口。

47 Japanese Bar（居酒屋）

Can I get you something to eat/drink?

要吃／喝點什麼？

green soybeans 毛豆	sushi 壽司	tofu 豆腐	mochi 麻糬
cheese 起司	sashimi 生魚片	mackerel 鯖魚	Japanese pancake 日式煎餅
fried tofu 炸豆腐	grilled fish 烤魚	stewed giblets 雜燴	yakitori 串燒雞肉
Japanese rolled omelet 日式煎蛋捲	beef and potato stew 馬鈴薯燉肉	veal cutlet 牛小排	fried dumplings 煎餃

katsu-don 豬排丼	unagi-don 鰻魚丼

We take last orders at 11 pm.

我們接受點餐至晚上11點。

Part 7 飲食

Useful Expressions 常用例句

1. Would you like to start with a cocktail? 您想要先喝杯雞尾酒嗎？
2. Would you like to see our wine list? 您要不要看一下我們的酒單？
3. Which brand of wine would you prefer?
   請問您要哪一個品牌的葡萄酒？
4. How about one of our nonalcoholic drinks?
   要不要來一杯不含酒精的飲料呢？
5. Have you made a choice? 您選好了嗎？
6. What is a Gin Fizz? 請問琴費士是什麼？
7. What does a Bloody Mary consist of?
   血腥瑪麗是用哪些酒調配而成的？
8. Do you have some pop? 你們有賣汽水嗎？
9. What brands of beer do you have? 你們有哪些牌子的啤酒？
10. I feel like having a glass of wine, please.
    我想要喝杯葡萄酒，謝謝。

Dialogue 實用對話

Bartender:	Would you care for a drink? 要喝點什麼嗎？
Guest:	A whiskey, please. 一杯威士忌，謝謝。
Bartender:	We have Scotch, Johnny Walker, and Irish. 我們有蘇格蘭威士忌、約翰走路和愛爾蘭威士忌。
Guest:	I'll take a Scotch whiskey. 我要一杯蘇格蘭威士忌。
Bartender:	How would you like it? 您要怎麼喝？
Guest:	On the rocks. 加冰塊。
Bartender:	Right away, Ms. 馬上來，小姐。

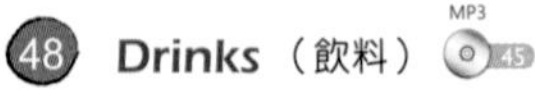

48 Drinks（飲料）

MP3 45

Bottoms up! 乾杯	Let's hit another bar. 我們到另一家酒吧去吧。

beer 啤酒	red wine 紅酒
sake 日本清酒	white wine 白酒
plum wine 梅酒	apricot wine 杏酒
cocktail 雞尾酒	whiskey 威士忌

juice 果汁	other drinks 其他飲料
grapefruit juice 葡萄柚汁	soda water 蘇打水
grape juice 葡萄汁	lemonade 檸檬水
apple juice 蘋果汁	lime juice 萊姆汁
Calpis 可爾必思	green tea 綠茶

Part 7 飲食

1. 常見酒類

whisky 威士忌	brandy 白蘭地	vodka 伏特加
gin 琴酒	rum 蘭姆酒	port 紅葡萄酒
tequila 龍舌蘭	bourbon 波本威士忌	sherry 雪莉酒
coolers 酒類果汁	cider 蘋果汁	beer 啤酒

2. 常見啤酒品牌

Sapporo 札幌啤酒	Heineken 海尼根	Corona 可樂娜
Budwiser 百威啤酒	Coors 酷爾斯啤酒	Becks 貝克啤酒
Molson Canadian 加拿大摩森啤酒	San Miguel 生力啤酒	Kirin 麒麟啤酒
Schlitz 施麗茲啤酒	Suntory 三多利啤酒	Guinness 金氏黑啤酒

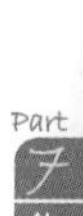

3. 點酒類時常見用語

on the rocks 加冰塊	large 大杯	medium 中杯	small 小杯
double 雙份	neat 純的	caffeine-free 不含咖啡因	
with soda water 加蘇打水		with plain water 加白開水	

Asian Food 1（亞洲食物 1）

Chinese cuisine 中國菜

	moo shu pork 木須肉
crab meat paste with tofu 蟹肉豆腐	braised pork 滷豬肉
wined shrimp 醉蝦	honey ham 蜜汁火腿
spiced diced chicken 辣子雞丁	sweet and sour spareribs 無錫排骨
spring rolls 春卷	hot and sour soup 酸辣湯

Japanese cuisine 日本料理

	pickled veggies 醬菜
natto 納豆	baked fish 烤魚
seaweed 海帶	miso soup 味噌湯
shichimi 七味辣椒粉	fried rice 炒飯
pickles 醬瓜	onigiri 飯糰

常見食材

1. 蔬菜

asparagus	蘆筍	bamboo shoot	竹筍	balsam pear	苦瓜
broccoli	綠花椰菜	cauliflower	花椰菜	carrot	胡蘿蔔
radish	白蘿蔔	cabbage	包心菜	celery	芹菜
cucumber	黃瓜	eggplant	茄子	onion	洋蔥
green pepper	青椒	lettuce	萵苣	potato	馬鈴薯
pumpkin	南瓜	spinach	菠菜	parsley	西洋芹
garlic	蒜	ginger	薑	green onion	青蔥

2. 肉類

beef	牛肉	pork	豬肉	mutton	羊肉
chicken	雞肉	duck	鴨肉	turkey	火雞
goose	鵝肉	veal	小牛肉	bacon	培根
sausage	香腸	hot dog	熱狗	fatty	肥肉

3. 海鮮

fish fillet	魚排	caviar	魚子醬	eel	鰻魚
squid	花枝	octopus	章魚	crab	螃蟹
clam	蛤蠣	lobster	龍蝦	shrimp	蝦
salmon	鮭魚	trout	鱒魚	oyster	牡蠣

50 Asian Food 2 （亞洲食物 2）

Thai food 泰國菜
grilled pork 烤豬肉
chicken satay with peanut sauce 雞肉沙嗲沾花生醬
seafood curry 海鮮咖哩

Indian dishes 印度料理
chapati 印度燒餅
Tandoori chicken 坦都烤雞
Indian milk tea 印度奶茶

Asian noodles 亞洲麵食		
rice noodles 米粉	flat noodles 板條	fried egg noodles 伊麵（油炸雞蛋麵）
soba 蕎麥麵	green bean noodles 冬粉	thin salted noodles 麵線
ramen 拉麵	fried noodles 炒麵	udon 烏龍麵

Useful Expressions 常用例句

This tastes good.

1. This tastes good. 真好吃！
2. This veal is tender. 這小牛肉很嫩。
3. This soup smells terrific.
   這湯聞起來真香。
4. This fried chicken is nice and crispy.
   這炸雞酥脆又好吃。
5. This bread is wonderful.
   這麵包非常好吃。
6. May I have some more bread, please?
   請再給我一些麵包。
7. Could you please bring me some more water?
   請幫我加水。
8. I dropped my fork. May I have another one?
   我的叉子掉了，可以換一支嗎？
9. Can you give me some more chili sauce?
   我還要一些辣椒醬。
10. May I have a container for the leftover food, please?
    可以幫我打包剩菜嗎？
11. Please clear away our table.
    請幫我們清理一下桌子。
12. Do you mind my taking some pictures in the restaurant?
    請問我可以在餐廳裡拍照嗎？
13. Where can I get some napkins and straws?
    請問哪裡有紙巾和吸管？

Part
7
飲
食

51 Hot Pot（火鍋） MP3 48

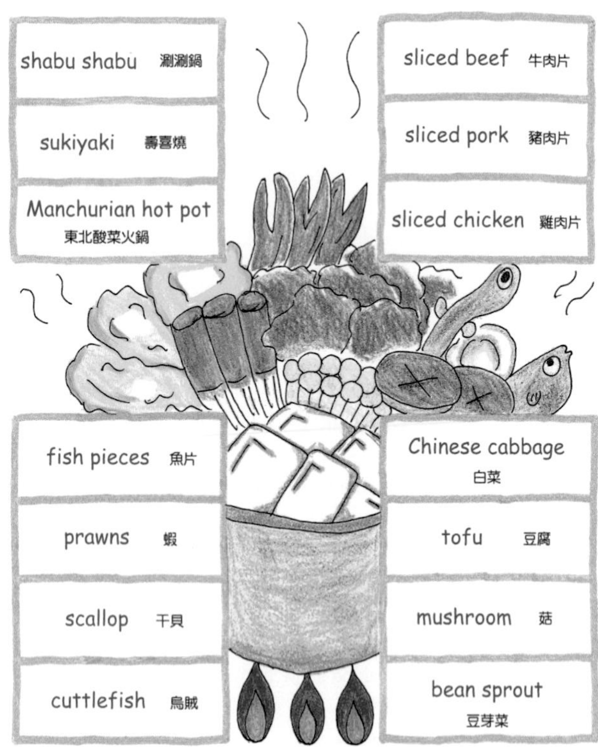

Part 7 飲食

Chinese Common Dishes （其他常見料理）

MP3

Yum Cha 飲茶

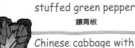

siu mai 燒賣	 fried wanton 炸餛飩
har gow 蝦餃	 fried rice cakes 炒年糕
	 spring rolls 春捲

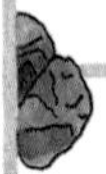

Chinese cuisine 中國菜

	rice cooked with soy sauce and pork 煲仔飯
 stuffed green pepper 鑲青椒	 steamed minced pork 蒸肉餅
Chinese cabbage with dried shrimp 開陽白菜	 mixed meat and seafood stew 佛跳牆
 cold pork 凍肉	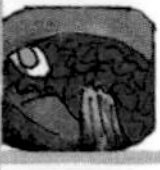 Sichuan hot noodles 擔擔麵
 various fried vegetables and egg 合菜帶帽	 fish fillet with rice wine sauce 糟溜魚片
 pig intestine in hotpot 五更腸旺	 abalone with oyster sauce 蠔油鮑片
tea smoked duck 樟茶鴨	 crispy chicken 脆皮炸子雞

53 Soups and Appetizers（湯品與配菜）

Would you like to start with a nice bowl of soup? 您要不要先點一碗湯？

vegetable soup 蔬菜湯	pumpkin soup 南瓜湯
potato soup 馬鈴薯湯	noodle soup 湯麵
French onion soup 法式洋蔥湯	minestrone 義大利蔬菜麵湯
lentil soup 扁豆湯	broth 肉湯
lobster soup 龍蝦湯	

salad 沙拉	butter 奶油
breadcrumbs 麵包粉	romaine lettuce 蘿蔓萵苣
cucumber 小黃瓜	fresh-ground black pepper 現磨黑胡椒
corn kernels 玉米粒	garlic 大蒜

各種湯類

soup	「湯」的通稱，一般我們在餐廳或家中喝到的湯，湯裡面可能會有各式各樣的配料。
broth	清湯，利用蔬菜、肉類或海鮮熬盛的湯頭，將所有殘渣過濾後得到的清湯，可以用來做各種湯品、醬料或濃湯。
stock	也是屬於作為湯底的清湯，但 stock 的原料是骨頭，而 broth 的原料主要為肉類。
gravy	通常指用於沾食的醬料，以肉汁為底，另外再加上高湯、酒、奶油等調味做成的醬汁，另外 gravy 也指單純的肉汁。

Dialogue 實用對話 W: Waitress G: Guest

W: Are you ready to order, sir.? 請問您要點餐了嗎，先生？

G: Yes, I want to start with an appetizer. What do you recommend? 是的，我要先點開胃菜，有什麼推薦的嗎？

W: The smoked beef is delicious. 煙燻牛肉非常美味。

G: The smoked beef sounds good. I'll try it. 煙燻牛肉聽起來不錯，我就試試看好了。

W: Would you like some soup? 請問您要喝湯嗎？

G: What do you have? 你們有哪些湯？

W: How about a bowl of vegetable soup or chicken broth? 來一碗蔬菜湯或清雞湯如何？

G: Vegetable soup, please. 那就蔬菜湯，謝謝。

W: All right. How about your main dish? 好的，那麼您的主餐呢？

G: I think I'll have a steak. 我想我點牛排好了。

W: Right. And to drink? 好的，那麼飲料呢？

G: Iced coffee, please. 冰咖啡，謝謝。

54 Sushi （壽司）

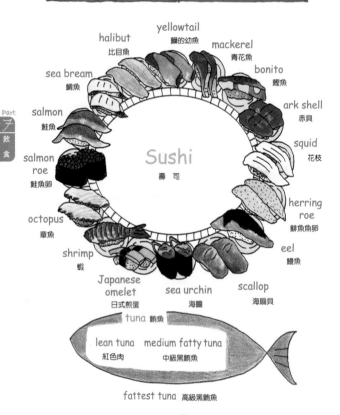

topping 上層餡料	filling 內餡

Sushi 壽司

yellowtail 鰤的幼魚
halibut 比目魚
mackerel 青花魚
sea bream 鯛魚
bonito 鰹魚
ark shell 赤貝
salmon 鮭魚
squid 花枝
salmon roe 鮭魚卵
herring roe 鯡魚魚卵
octopus 章魚
eel 鰻魚
shrimp 蝦
Japanese omelet 日式煎蛋
sea urchin 海膽
scallop 海扇貝

tuna 鮪魚

lean tuna 紅色肉
medium fatty tuna 中級黑鮪魚
fattest tuna 高級黑鮪魚

日本料理

sushi	壽司，以醋飯及芥末為主要食材，上面覆蓋生魚片或以海苔包裹醋飯及內餡。
nigirizushi	握壽司，是將醋飯捏成小口，再於上方覆蓋生魚片及芥末而成。
makizushi	壽司捲，包裹各種的捲式壽司，例：小黃瓜捲、鮪魚捲。
north American style rolls	北美式的壽司，例如： 1. 加州壽司捲（California roll）：材料包含酪梨、蟹肉、蔬菜等。 2. 龍壽司（ Dragon roll ）：材料包括鰻魚、酪梨等。 3. 蜘蛛壽司（ Spider roll）：內餡包括有炸軟殼蟹肉和酪梨等。 「龍壽司」及「蜘蛛壽司」等是美式日本料理菜單，與日本當地傳統的壽司使用食材不同，名稱也很特別。
futomaki	太卷，粗的壽司捲（用一張海苔捲的是「太卷」；用半張海苔捲的是「細卷」）
sashimi	生魚片，生的魚肉切片，沾醬油及芥末食用。 例：鰤魚類、鮪魚、章魚、海膽、蝦子、鮭魚卵
shioyaki	鹽烤，加上鹽巴燒烤的食物。例：鹽烤鯖魚
udon	烏龍麵：粗的、有嚼勁的白麵條。

yakiudon	炒麵，炒的麵條。
soba	蕎麥麵，利用蕎麥做的麵條（多沾日本式清淡的醬油，吃冷的）
ramen	拉麵，小麥麵粉做的麵，通常拿來煮湯麵。
tempura	天婦羅，炸蔬菜和海鮮。例：鮮蝦天婦羅、蔬菜天婦羅
donburi/ don	丼，一個大碗裡面有裝米飯，飯上放上食材。 例：豬排丼（飯上放炸豬排）、親子丼（飯上放雞肉及蛋）、 鰻魚丼（飯上放烤鰻魚）、牛肉丼（飯上放牛肉）。

55 Western Style Food（西餐）

MP3 

cheese omelet	起司煎蛋捲	potato salad	馬鈴薯沙拉
triple meat omelet	三層肉煎蛋捲	vegetable sandwich	蔬菜三明治
steak	牛排	hash brown	薯餅
pizza	披薩	chicken noodles	雞肉麵湯
roast beef	烤牛肉	chicken sausage pilaf	雞肉香腸燉肉飯
baked potato	烤馬鈴薯	clam chowder	蛤蠣巧達湯
chicken salad	雞肉沙拉		

	fried shrimp 炸蝦	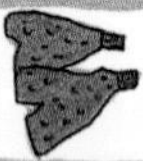	fried fillet 炸魚排

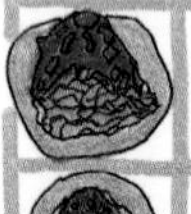	spaghetti with tomato sauce 番茄義大利麵		fettuccine Alfredo 奶油醬義大利麵
	spaghetti with meat sauce 肉醬義大利麵		pesto pasta with chicken 雞肉青醬義大利麵

Dialogue 實用對話 W: Waiter G: Guest

W: May I take your order, madam?

G: Yes, I'll take sirloin steak.

W: How would you like your steak—rare, medium, or well-done?

G: Medium, please. What comes with the sirloin steak?

W: Baked potato or onion rings?

G: Baked potato, please.

W: How about a salad, madam?

G: Yes. What do you have?

W: Our garden salad is very good.

G: A garden salad sounds good. I'll have that.

W: And what would you like to drink after your meal?

G: I would like a cup of espresso.

W: OK. I'll be back with your order.

W：請問要點餐了嗎，小姐？

G：是的，我要點沙朗牛排。

W：請問您的牛排要幾分熟？三分熟、五分熟還是全熟？

G：五分熟，請問牛排的附餐是什麼？

W：可以選烤馬鈴薯或洋蔥圈。

G：烤馬鈴薯，謝謝。

W：要吃一點沙拉嗎？

G：好的，你們有些什麼沙拉？

W：我們的田園沙拉很不錯。

G：田園沙拉聽起來不錯，就點田園沙拉。

W：那麼您的餐後飲料是？

G：我要一杯濃縮咖啡。

W：好的，您的餐點馬上就來。

56 Coffee/Tea （咖啡／茶）

Can I have a refill, please? 請問我可以續杯嗎？

Sure. Here you go. 當然，這是您的飲料。

COFFEE		TEA	
americano	美式咖啡	milk tea	奶茶
blended coffee	特調咖啡	Assam tea	阿薩姆茶
espresso	濃縮咖啡	Earl Grey tea	伯爵茶
cappuccino	卡布奇諾	Darjeeling tea	大吉嶺
mocha	摩卡咖啡	Russian Caravan	俄國茶
latte	拿鐵咖啡	English breakfast tea	英式早餐茶
iced vanilla latte	冰香草拿鐵咖啡	Nilgiri tea	尼爾吉里茶

OTHER			
hot chocolate	熱巧克力	vanilla	香草
cinnamon	肉桂	caramel	焦糖

下午茶

Afternoon tea	一般所說的下午茶主要是在下午三、四點左右食用的飲料和點心，包括一壺茶和以三層點心架擺放的小點心，例如三明治、烤圓餅、火腿、燻鮭魚，以及一些餅乾點心。在下午茶時間人們會以精緻的瓷器飲茶、品嚐點心，悠閒地聊天，享受一天之中輕鬆愉快的時光。
High tea	high tea在英國及愛爾蘭地區是指接近傍晚時所食用的餐點，食物較一般的下午茶多，包括三明治、蛋糕、點心和水果等，可以取代正式的晚餐，用來填飽肚子。

Useful Expressions 常用例句

1. Could you pass me the sugar, please?
   請你把糖遞給我好嗎？
2. What kind of tea is it? 這是什麼茶？
3. Where is this tea from?
   這是哪裡產的茶？
4. Do you serve English breakfast tea here?
   你們有英國早餐茶嗎？
5. Does this tea go well with a slice of lemon?
   這種茶加檸檬好喝嗎？
6. What's in the sandwich?
   這三明治裡夾什麼？
7. Could you add some hot water to the pot?
   麻煩你在茶壺裡加熱水好嗎？
8. What are the hours for afternoon tea?
   喝下午茶的時間是什麼時候？
9. What kind of cake goes well with Assam tea?
   阿薩姆茶配什麼蛋糕好呢？
10. Can I take a look at the tea menu? 讓我看一下茶單好嗎？

Desserts （甜點）

Can I have another piece of chocolate cake?
我可以再吃一塊巧克力蛋糕嗎？

ice cream 冰淇淋	cheese cake 起司蛋糕
yogurt 優格	strawberry tart 草莓蛋糕
crepe 可麗餅	tiramisu 提拉米蘇
mousse 慕斯	chestnut cake 栗子蛋糕
sundae 聖代	oatmeal cookie 燕麥餅乾
pudding 布丁	cream puff 泡芙
pie 派	banana split 香蕉船
peanut butter 花生醬	Jello 果凍
pancake/waffle 鬆餅	popcorn 爆米花

pancake 煎餅
waffle 網格狀鬆餅

Part 7 飲食

58 Fruits （水果） MP3 55

cantaloupe	哈密瓜	strawberry	草莓
orange	柳橙	tangerine	橘子
peach	桃子	cherry	櫻桃
watermelon	西瓜	pear	梨
persimmon	柿子	passionfruit	百香果
grape	葡萄	banana	香蕉
papaya	木瓜	mango	芒果

一些被我們視為蔬菜的食材其實屬於水果，例如：南瓜（pumpkin）、小黃瓜（cucumber）、茄子（eggplant）等，而番茄則既被視為蔬菜也是水果。

Part 7 飲食

Seasoning （調味料）

salt 鹽	soy sauce 醬油
vegetable oil 蔬菜油	vinegar 醋
pepper 胡椒	chili sauce 辣椒醬
syrup 楓糖漿	sugar 糖
mustard 芥末	ketchup 番茄醬
spice 香料	flavor 香味／味道
garlic 蒜	ginger 薑
onion 洋蔥	clove 丁香
nutmeg 豆蔻	parsley 荷蘭芹
salad dressing 沙拉醬	steak sauce 牛排醬

食物的烹調方式

西餐廳的食物烹調方法有許多種，出國點餐時會在菜單上見到不同的食物調理方式，為免點錯自己要吃的食物，最好先熟悉一下烹調食物正確的英文用法。

braise	燜，在鍋中放少許油和水，蓋上蓋子後慢慢地燜，一般用於烹煮肉類。
roast	烤，通常用於一大塊烤肉，可能在烤箱中或是在爐火上烤。
grill/ broil	烤，grilled 和 roasted 不同之處在於，grilled 以食物直接接觸火，一般是放在烤架上烤。（grilled 是美式用法，broiled 則是英式用法）
barbecue	以木炭燒烤，一般在野外烤肉就被稱作 barbecue。
fry	油炸，大量的油以火燒滾後，將食物放進油裡炸。
stir fry	拌炒，屬於中式的炒菜法。
saute	嫩煎，在鍋中加入少許油脂加熱，將食物放進去煎。
stew	燉，加水用文火久煮使爛熟，多用於燉煮肉類。
boil	用水煮沸，但煮熟後只吃被煮的食物，不會去喝湯。
steam	蒸，以蒸汽將食物燜熟。

Part 7 飲食

 60 Special Request on Food（特別要求）

No onion, please. 不要加洋蔥，謝謝。
I am allergic to seafood. 我對海鮮過敏。
I like my eggs soft. 我的蛋要半熟。

	sunny side up 荷包蛋（只煎一面）		dairy product 乳製品
	wheat flour 小麥粉		squid ink spaghetti 墨魚麵
	bean(s) 豆類		sweet potato 蕃薯
	fruit 水果	refreshments 點心；茶點	

Guest:	Do you serve vegetarian food?
Waitress:	Yes, we serve vegetarian food everyday from 11 am to 10 pm.

顧　客：請問你們有提供素食餐點嗎？

服務生：有的，我們每天上午十一點到晚上十點都有提供素食。

Useful Expressions 實用例句

1. Do you have vegetarian food? 你們有素食餐點嗎？

2. I am a vegan. 我吃全素。

> vegetarian（蛋奶素）是指不吃肉類及海鮮的素食者，但還是會吃乳製品或蛋類，而 vegan 則是連乳製品和蛋都不吃的全素食。

3. Are these vegetables grown organically?
   這些蔬菜都是有機栽培的嗎？

4. Does your restaurant have a dress code?
   到你們餐廳吃飯有規定衣著嗎？

   Yes, we have a formal dress code. Gentlemen are requested to wear a tie. Jeans or sandals are not permitted in our restaurant. 是的，我們有正式的衣著規定。男士必須打領帶，而牛仔褲和涼鞋都是不被允許的。

5. I don't eat red meat.
   我不吃紅肉。

6. I'm allergic to shellfish.
   我對貝類過敏。

7. Excuse me. What's this knife for?
   請問這把刀子是用來做什麼的？

   It's a salad knife. You can use it to cut your salad.
   這是沙拉刀，您可以用來切沙拉。

8. Do I eat it with a spoon?
   這道菜我要用湯匙吃嗎？

Dining （飲食）

eating with chopsticks 用筷子吃	heat up 加熱
bar counter 酒吧吧台	microwave meal 微波食物
table for four 四人座	service fee 服務費
seat by the window 靠窗的座位	cover charge 入場費
tatami room 榻榻米的房間	buffet 自助餐吃到飽
take-out food 外帶食物	extra large 特大
appetizer 開胃菜	main course 主餐
Today's special 今日特餐	gourmet 美食家
share dishes 吃合菜	box 包廂
service 服務品質	free of charge 不收費

Supplementary Vocabulary 單字補充

bill/check 帳單	clear the table 清理桌子	salad bar 沙拉吧
set the table 將桌子餐具準備好	foodstall 小吃攤	appetite 胃口
overcooked 過熟	undercooked 沒煮熟	beverage 飲料
alcohol 酒精飲料	freshwater fish 淡水魚	saltwater fish 海水魚

Dialogue 實用對話

Guest: Can I see the menu, please?
可以給我菜單嗎？

Waiter: Certainly. Here you are. 當然，這是菜單。

Guest: Do you have a set lunch? 請問你們有午餐套餐嗎？

Waiter: I am sorry. Not on Saturdays. 很抱歉，週六沒有供應。

Guest: In that case, I'd like a Caesar salad and an iced coffee.
這樣的話，我要一份凱薩沙拉和一杯冰咖啡。

62 Asking for Directions 1 （問路 1）

Could you tell me how to get to the Tourist Information Center? 可以麻煩你告訴我觀光詢問處要怎麼走嗎？

Go straight along the road, and turn right at the first intersection. You'll see it on the right. 沿著這條路直走，在第一個路口右轉，就在右手邊。

Where should I get off for the multiplex?
請問到影城要在哪一站下車？

You should get off at the next stop.
你應該要在下一站下車。

Excuse me. Which bus goes to Sea World?
請問一下，到海洋世界要搭哪一班車？

You can take route No. 12. It comes every fifteen minutes.
你可以搭12號公車，每15分鐘一班。

Can I get there on foot? 走路可以到嗎？

Yes, it's a ten-minute's walk. 可以，大概走10分鐘。

Is the airport far from here? 機場離這裡很遠嗎？

Yes, it's about two miles from here. You'd better get a taxi. 是，離這裡大約兩英哩，你最好搭計程車。

Can you tell me where I can find a bank?
不好意思，可以告訴我哪裡有銀行嗎？

Oh. A branch of Central State Bank is located on the second floor of that building. 啊，州立銀行分行就在那棟大樓的二樓。

Excuse me. Could you point out where it is on the map?
不好意思，可以請你指出這裡在地圖上的哪個地方嗎？

Sure. Can I see the map? 沒問題，讓我看一下地圖好嗎？

Dialogue 1 實用對話 1

Where's the main branch of the city's library, please?
請問市立圖書館的分館在哪裡？

It's in Grand Avenue, near the National Historical Museum.
在格蘭德大道上，靠近國家歷史博物館。

Is it far away from here? 離這裡遠嗎？

No, it's only about 500 meters. You can walk there in 5 minutes. 不遠，離這裡大約五百公尺，五分鐘就走到了。

Dialogue 2 實用對話 2

Excuse me, should I get off here for Union Park?
對不起，請問到聯合公園是在這裡下車嗎？

Yes. After you get off, turn right and walk for a few minutes and then you'll be there. 對。你下車後先右轉，走個幾分鐘就到了。

Thank you very much indeed. 真是謝謝你。

You're welcome. 不客氣。

63 Asking for Directions 2 （問路 2）

MP3 60

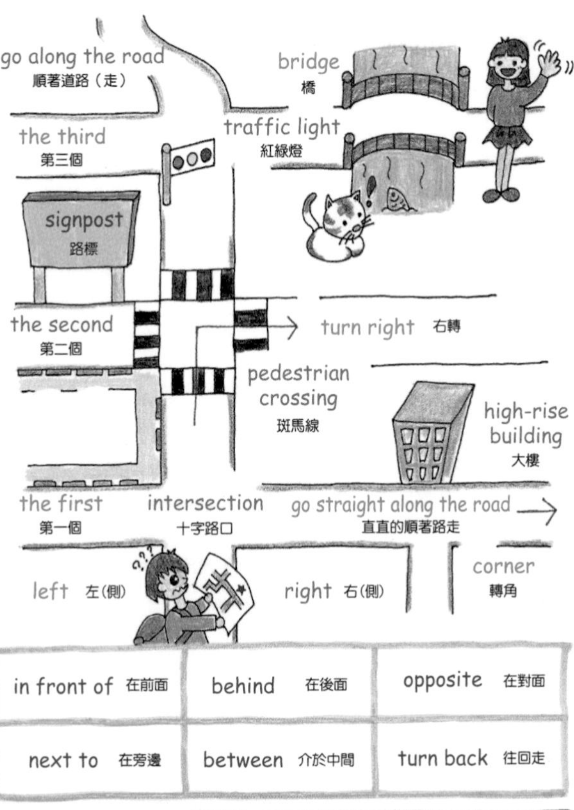

in front of 在前面	behind 在後面	opposite 在對面
next to 在旁邊	between 介於中間	turn back 往回走

Thank you for your help. 謝謝你的幫忙。

Supplementary Vocabulary 單字補充

sidewalk 人行道	streetlight 路燈	phone booth 電話亭	road 馬路
underpass 地下道	handrail 扶手	crosswalk 行人穿越道	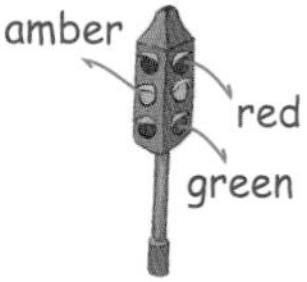
traffic light 紅綠燈	stop sign 停止路標	pedestrian bridge 天橋	street sign 路標

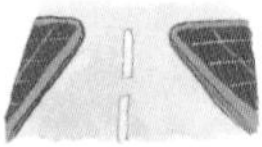

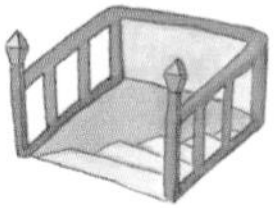

amber
red
green

STOP

Useful Expressions 表達謝意的說法

1. That's nice of you. Thank you. 你真好，謝謝你。
2. Thank you. I appreciate it. 謝謝你，我很感激。
3. That would be a great help. Thank you. 那真是幫了大忙了。謝謝。
4. I'm much obliged to you for your help. 非常感謝您的幫忙。
5. It's nice of you to help. 你能幫忙真好。

 Holidays and Festivals （節慶假日） 

MP3 61

- New Year's Day ………… 新年（1月1日）
- Martin Luther King Day ‥ 馬丁路德金恩紀念日（1月的第三個星期一）
- Valentine's Day ………… 西洋情人節（2月14日）
- St. Patrick's Day ………… 聖派翠克節（3月17日）
- Easter ………… 復活節（3月底至四月下旬間）
- April Fool's Day ………… 愚人節（4月1日）
- May Day ………… 五朔節（5月1日）
- Mother's Day ………… 母親節（5月的第二個星期天）
- Memorial Day ………… 陣亡將士紀念日（5月的最後一個星期一）
- Father's Day ………… 父親節（8月8日）
- Independence Day ………（美國）獨立紀念日（7月4日）
- Labor Day ………… 勞動節（9月的第一個星期一）
- Columbus Day ………… 哥倫布（登陸美洲）紀念日（10月的第二個星期一）
- Halloween ………… 萬聖節（10月31日）
- Veteran's Day ………（美國）退伍軍人節（11月11日）
- Thanksgiving Day ………… 感恩節（11月的第四個星期四）
- Christmas Day ………… 聖誕節（12月25日）

Spring 春

warm air 暖和的空氣
new life 新生
spring fever 春季懶洋洋的情緒

Summer 夏

high summer 盛夏
outdoor activity 戶外活動
ice cream 冰淇淋

Fall/Autumn 秋

maple leaves 楓（葉）
harvest 收成

autumn foliage 秋季落葉季節

Winter 冬

skating 溜冰
rink 溜冰場
snowball fight 打雪球戰

Public Holidays in Taiwan 我國的重要節日

- Chinese New Year's Eve 除夕
- Chinese New Year 農曆新年
- the Lantern Festival 元宵節（農曆1月15日）
- Peace Memorial Day 和平紀念日（2月28日）
- Youth Day 青年節（3月29日）
- Tomb Sweeping Day 清明節（4月5日）
- Labor Day 勞動節（5月1日）
- Dragon Boat Festival 端午節（農曆5月5日）
- Mid-Autumn Festival 中秋節（農曆8月15日）
- Teachers' Day 教師節（9月28日）
- Double Tenth Day 雙十節（10月10日）
- Constitution Day 行憲紀念日（12月25日）

Useful Expressions 實用例句

1. Chinese New Year falls on January 1 in the lunar calendar.
   農曆新年是每年農曆的一月一日。
2. Eating sweet dumplings is probably the most fun thing you can do while celebrating the Lantern Festival.
   吃湯圓應該算是慶祝元宵節最有趣的部分。
3. Tomb Sweeping Day is the day for Chinese people to remember their ancestors. 清明節是中國人懷念祖先的日子。
4. Dragon boat racing is the most important event during a Dragon Boat Festival. 龍舟賽是端午節最重要的活動。
5. The traditional Mid-Autumn Festival food is the moon cake.
   中秋節要吃的傳統食物是月餅。
6. Double Tenth Day is celebrated not only by people in Taiwan, but also by many overseas Chinese.
   不只台灣人會慶祝雙十節，許多海外華僑也會慶祝。

65 Christmas （聖誕節）

festival 慶典；節慶	Christmas 聖誕節	Santa Claus 聖誕老人
mistletoe 槲寄生	Christmas tree 聖誕樹	present 禮物

reindeer 麋鹿	Christmas carols 聖誕歌曲	sleigh 雪橇
snowman 雪人	chimney 煙囪	fireplace 火爐

聖誕老人（Santa Claus）的由來

聖誕老人原本是住在土耳其的一位主教，他真正的名字是尼可拉斯（Nicholas）。他之所以聞名，是因為他常熱心幫助有需要的孩童：他會穿著紅色或白色的長袍，戴上一頂又高又尖的帽子，到各個城鄉地區帶領大家遊行，和小孩聊天，並送小禮物給他們。在他死後的一段時間，他被設定為小孩的守護神。

他過世的日子是12月6日，這天在歐洲的某些國家也成了節日。為了歡渡聖．尼可拉斯（St. Nicholas）節慶，這些國家的小孩會在12月5日的晚上拿出鞋子或掛起襪子，然後在隔天早上醒來時，會去找鞋子和襪子裡的禮物。後來此節日和聖誕節一起慶祝。紐約市的荷蘭移民把這項習俗帶到新世界，並把聖尼可拉斯的荷蘭文 Sinterklaas 改成了英文的 Santa Claus。

Supplementary Vocabulary 單字補充

celebration 慶祝	tradition 傳統	throw a party 舉辦派對
New Year's resolutions 新年願望		blessing 祝福
parade 遊行	carnival 嘉年華	Easter egg 復活節彩蛋
firework 煙火	Halloween 萬聖節	trick or treat 不給糖就搗蛋
pumpkin 南瓜	Jack-o-lantern 南瓜燈	costume 戲服
Thanksgiving dinner 感恩節晚餐		turkey 火雞
feast 盛宴	ornament 裝飾	ribbon 緞帶

Merry Christmas! 聖誕快樂！

Happy New Year! 新年快樂！

What is your New Year's resolution? 你的新年願望是什麼？

66 Baseball （看棒球）

infield seat/outfield seat 內野／外野觀眾席	grandstand/bleachers 正面／露天看臺
pitcher 投手	batter 打擊手
baseball gloves 棒球手套	bat 球棒
baseball fan 棒球球迷	home run 全壘打

美國的職棒聯盟隊伍：目前美國職棒聯盟中十六隊屬國家聯盟，十四隊屬美國聯盟，以下列舉部分隊伍：

Atlanta Braves 亞特蘭大勇士隊	Chicago Cubs 芝加哥小熊隊
New York Mets 紐約大都會隊	Pittsburgh Pirates 匹茲堡海盜隊
Philadelphia Phillies 費城費城人隊	Colorado Rockies 科羅拉多洛磯隊
Los Angeles Dodgers 洛杉磯道奇隊	Boston Red Sox 波士頓紅襪隊
San Francisco Giants 舊金山巨人隊	New York Yankees 紐約洋基隊
Detroit Tigers 底特律老虎隊	Chicago White Sox 芝加哥白襪隊
Seattle Mariners 西雅圖水手隊	Texas Rangers 德州遊騎兵隊

Other Sports 其他運動

backboard 籃板
basket 籃框
shoot a basket 投籃得分
dribble 運球
basketball 籃球

net 網
tennis racquet 網球拍
grass court 草地球場
tennis 網球

football 足球
run 跑
kick 踢

volleyball 排球
pass 傳球
serve 發球

67 Amusement Park （遊樂園）

I want to ride the roller coaster.
我想坐雲霄飛車。

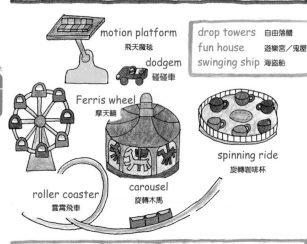

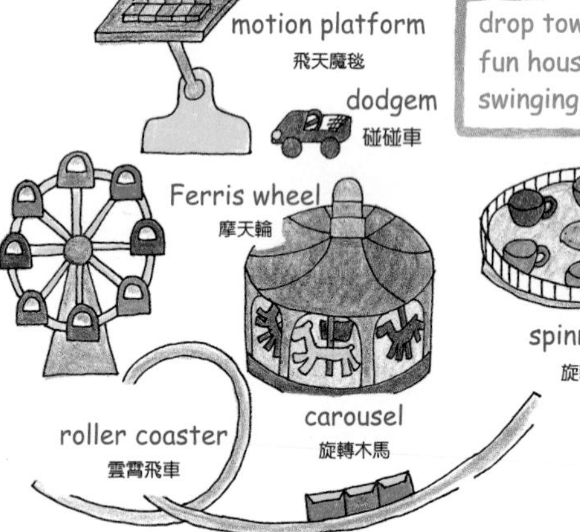

drop towers	自由落體
fun house	遊樂宮／鬼屋
swinging ship	海盜船

theme park　主題樂園	admission charge　入場費
funfair　遊樂園	queue　排隊

What time does Universal Studios open?
環球影城幾點開門？

Two tickets for adults and two for children, please.
請給我兩張全票、兩張兒童票。

Amusement Park 遊樂園

Amusement Park 是指擁有多項遊樂設施的娛樂場所，
國內外旅遊景點往往都有各種不同的遊樂園，主要分為以下幾種：

Theme Park 主題樂園	所有遊樂設施都有同樣主題的遊樂園，例如以電影情節為主題的加州環球影城（Universal Studios Theme Park），園區內所有的遊樂設施都是環球電影公司所拍攝的電影為主要內容。
Funfair 露天遊樂園	funfair 同樣為遊樂園，但是場地和設施都是可以拆卸移動的，往往在各地巡迴，因此可能在同一個地區停留幾天後便遷移。
Water Park 水上樂園	以水上遊樂設施為主的遊樂園，除了戶外的水上樂園，世界各地也有不少建在室內的水上樂園，讓遊客即使不在海邊也能享受玩水的樂趣。

Useful Expressions 常用例句

1. Where is the ticket booth?
   請問售票處在哪裡？
2. How much does it cost for admission?
   請問入場券多少錢？
3. I'd like two tickets for adults and three for children, please.
   我要兩張全票，三張兒童票。
4. Does the admission include everything?
   請問是一票玩到底嗎？
5. What is the most popular ride in Disneyland?
   迪士尼樂園裡最受歡迎的是哪一項設施？
6. Is this the line for the extreme roller coaster?
   請問這個隊伍是排終極雲霄飛車嗎？
7. I lost my bag in the haunted house.
   我的背包掉在鬼屋裡了。
8. I lost the key to the locker.
   我把寄物櫃的鑰匙弄丟了。

 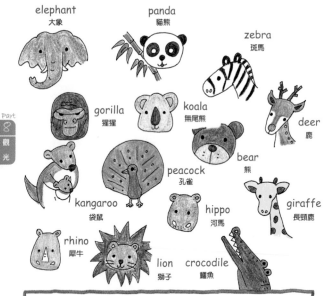 Zoo （動物園） 

elephant 大象

panda 貓熊

zebra 斑馬

gorilla 猩猩

koala 無尾熊

deer 鹿

bear 熊

peacock 孔雀

kangaroo 袋鼠

hippo 河馬

giraffe 長頸鹿

rhino 犀牛

lion 獅子

crocodile 鱷魚

Would you please take a picture for me?
可以請你幫我拍張照嗎？

Please don't feed the animals. 請不要餵食動物。

Wash your hands after you have contacted with animals.
接觸過動物後請記得洗手。

Do not cross the barrier. 請勿越過柵欄。

Supplementary Vocabulary 認識更多動物

alpaca	羊駝	camel	駱駝	armadillo	犰狳
ape	大猩猩	baboon	狒狒	caterpillar	毛毛蟲
eagle	老鷹	bat	蝙蝠	fox	狐狸
coyote	郊狼	crane	鶴	ferret	雪貂
hare	野兔	hawk	鷹	hyena	土狼
leopard	美洲豹	monkey	猴子	horse	馬
mule	騾	polar bear	北極熊	sheep	綿羊
spider	蜘蛛	squirrel	松鼠	alligator	短吻鱷
tiger	老虎	swan	天鵝	turtle	海龜
toad	蟾蜍	frog	青蛙	wolf	狼

Useful Expressions 實用例句

1. Will there be a big crowd on the weekend? 週末會不會很多人？
2. Where can I see some interesting animal shows?
   請問哪裡有好看的動物演出？
3. When will the show finish? 請問表演幾點結束？
4. May I leave my coat here? 我可以把外套寄放在這兒嗎？
5. May I take photos during the show? 請問看表演時可以拍照嗎？

69 Aquarium （水族館）

MP3 66

The dolphin show starts at 2 p.m.
海豚秀是從下午2點開始。

Sea World 海洋公園

Sea World 是美國最著名的連鎖遊樂園，園內以展示各種海生動物以及表演為主題，吸引遊客前來，代表動物是一隻殺人鯨。目前全美共有三間 **Sea World**，分別在佛羅里達州的奧蘭多、加州的聖地牙哥，以及德州的聖安東尼奧。除了海洋動物的展示與表演外，園區內另外也設有一般的遊樂設施如雲霄飛車等，有機會前往這幾個地區時也可以一遊海洋公園，感受海底生物的魅力。

Supplementary Vocabulary 單字補充

mammal	哺乳動物	reptile	爬蟲類	pet	寵物
cage	籠子	fish tank	魚缸	snake	蛇
predator	肉食性動物	prey	獵物	frog	青蛙
jellyfish	水母	starfish	海星	insect	昆蟲
spider	蜘蛛	moth	飛蛾	cricket	蟋蟀
grasshopper	蚱蜢	butterfly	蝴蝶	feather	羽毛
tail	尾巴	beak	喙	horn	角

70 Religious Buildings（教堂與寺廟）

MP3 

church 教堂

cathedral 大教堂	mosque 清真寺
nun 修女	monk 僧侶
monastery 修道院	altar 祭壇

各種不同的宗教集會場所

1. church 教堂：是指基督徒崇拜上帝的聚會場所，也是平日最常使用的用語。
2. chapel 小禮拜堂：與教堂同樣為基督徒崇拜上帝或做禮拜的場所，但場地較小，往往附屬於教堂（church）之下。
3. cathedral 大教堂：同樣為教堂，但建築較一般教堂雄偉寬敞，地位也比較重要。
4. mosque 清真寺：回教徒進行宗教儀式的主要會所，如同基督徒做禮拜的教堂。
5. synagogue 猶太徒會所：猶太教教徒做禮拜的地方。
6. Buddhist temple 佛寺：佛教徒進行宗教儀式、祈求祝福的會所。

Christianity 基督教	Catholicity 天主教
Buddhism 佛教	Muslim 回教
Hindu 印度教	Taoism 道教
cross 十字架	pray 祈禱
worship 崇拜	ritual 儀式

Useful Expressions 常用例句

1. Are there any interesting places to see here?
這裡有什麼好玩的地方？

2. What is the most famous historical building in the city?
這個城市最有名的建築是什麼呢？

3. Is St. Paul's Cathedral open on Sundays?
請問聖保羅教堂星期天有開放嗎？

4. Do you have a brochure for the tour to Notre Dame?
請問你們有介紹遊聖母院的手冊嗎？

5. I'd like to sign up for the tour of Canterbury Cathedral.
我想預約坎特伯里教堂的旅遊行程。

71 Hot Spring （溫泉） MP3 

It is said that thermal water from a hot spring is good for your health. 據說溫泉水對能讓身體健康。

spa 溫泉療養	geothermal 地熱
groundwater 地下水	temperature 溫度
steam 蒸汽	mud pot 泥漿泉
cold spring 冷泉	therapeutic uses 醫療效用
volcanic activity 火山活動	boiling point 沸點

therapeutic effect 療效	
respiratory failure 呼吸疾病	skin problem 皮膚病
wound 外傷	acne 面皰／粉刺
infection 感染	gout 痛風
hypertension/ high blood pressure 高血壓	muscle ache 肌肉痠痛
skin whitening 美白肌膚	headache 頭痛

Useful Expressions
實用例句

Could you please recommend some hot spring resorts? 可以請你推薦一些溫泉休閒中心嗎？

What are the open hours of the hot spring pool?
請問溫泉池的開放時間是？

Could you please bring me one more bath towel?
可以麻煩你再給我一條浴巾嗎？

Can we have our meals in our room?
我們可以在房間裡用餐嗎？

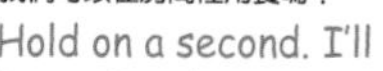

Hold on a second. I'll put you through to Room Service. 請稍等，我為您轉接到客房服務。

泡溫泉的方法

1. 溫泉因為是共用的，所以下去泡之前要先將身體洗乾淨。
2. 嚴禁將自己帶來的毛巾浸到溫泉水裡，把毛巾放在頭上泡湯。
3. 泡湯時間依溫泉種類而不同，但第一次最好是3～10分鐘左右，習慣後再慢慢延長時間。而泡湯的次數一天2～3次為最適當。
4. 避免因沖洗而造成溫泉物質的流失，讓溫泉裡對身體好的物質，一點一點的從皮膚滲透到體內，所以泡湯後避免用水直接沖洗身體，當然易過敏體質的人另當別論。
5. 有以下症狀時應避免泡湯：
   - 急性疾病（特別是發燒時）
   - 開放性肺結核患者
   - 惡性腫瘤
   - 有呼吸障礙的患者
   - 腎功能不全的患者
   - 嚴重貧血的患者
   - 具出血性疾病的患者
   - 孕婦
   - 其他一般病人
   - 重大心臟病患者

72 Galleries/Museums （美術館／博物館）

MP3

You are not allowed to take pictures in the museum.
博物館中禁止照相。

Please don't touch the paintings.
請勿觸碰畫作。

No talking in the gallery.
畫廊中請勿交談。

No food or drinks are allowed.
請勿飲食。

Part 8 觀光

Do you have a Chinese-speaking tour guide?
請問有中文的導覽嗎？

What is on exhibition at the art gallery?
請問藝廊正在展覽什麼？

When is the next guided tour?
請問下次導覽是什麼時候？

exhibit 展覽

artistic work 藝術作品

art studio
藝術工作室

calligraphy 書法

artist 藝術家

art gallery
美術展覽館

library reading room
圖書館閱覽室

access and facilities for disabled people
無障礙空間及設施

Supplementary Vocabulary 單字補充

aesthetics	美學	pottery	陶藝	fresco	壁畫
collection	館藏	photography	攝影	original	真跡
replica	複製品	sculpture	雕刻	paintbrush	畫筆
videotape	錄影	postcard	明信片	poster	海報

Useful Expressions 常用例句

1. How long will the exhibit continue?
這次的展覽會展出多久？

2. Is there an admission fee?
要入場費嗎？

3. Where can I buy a ticket?
請問我要到哪裡買票？

4. When is the museum open?
博物館何時開放？

5. When is the next Chinese language tour?
下一次中文導覽是什麼時候？

6. Could you give me a floor map of the exhibition?
可以請你給我一張導覽圖嗎？

7. Can I take pictures with a flash?
請問我可以用閃光燈拍照嗎？

8. Where can I buy postcards of the art works in this exhibition?
請問哪裡可以買到展覽品的明信片？

9. I'd like to see the modern sculptures.
我想要看當代的雕刻作品。

10. Do you have a Chinese edition of this book?
請問這本書有中文版嗎？

73 Outdoor Activities （戶外活動）

MP3 

sunrise 黎明

sunset 日落

Part 8 觀光

mountain 山

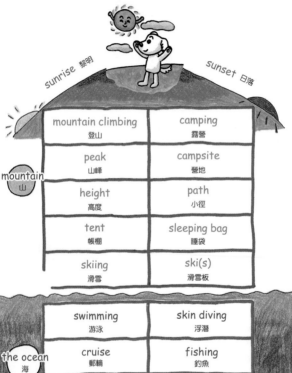

mountain climbing 登山	camping 露營
peak 山峰	campsite 營地
height 高度	path 小徑
tent 帳棚	sleeping bag 睡袋
skiing 滑雪	ski(s) 滑雪板

the ocean 海

swimming 游泳	skin diving 浮潛
cruise 郵輪	fishing 釣魚
swimsuit 泳衣	surfing 衝浪
beach 海灘	scuba diving 潛水

Supplementary Vocabulary 單字補充

outdoorsman/outdoorswoman 愛好戶外活動者		
bungee jumping 高空彈跳	cycling 騎越野車	ice skating 溜冰
beach volleyball 沙灘排球	jogging 慢跑	horse riding 騎馬
hiking 健行	parachuting 跳傘	backpack 背包
motor home 露營車	trailer 活動拖車	canoe 獨木舟
paddle 船槳	fishing rod 釣竿	fishing line 釣線
waterfall 瀑布	brook 小溪	wilderness 野外
compass 指南針	flashlight 手電筒	portable stove 火爐

Useful Expressions 常用例句

1. Is there a nice golf course near here?
   這附近有不錯的高爾夫球場嗎？
2. I've always wanted to try bungee jumping.
   我一直都想試試看高空彈跳。
3. What kind of marine sports can we do at this beach?
   我們在這個海灘可以做什麼水上運動？
4. I'd like to try canoeing.
   我想要試試划獨木舟。
5. Where can I rent ski equipment?
   請問我要去哪裡租滑雪器具？

 Making Phone Calls 1 （打電話 1） 

- Excuse me. Where is a public phone?
  請問哪裡有公共電話？

- Where do you put the phone card?
  請問電話卡要插哪裡？

- Can I leave a message?
  我可以留言嗎？

- Can I make an international call on this telephone?
  我可以用這個打國際電話嗎？

- Where can I get a phone book?
  哪裡可以找到電話簿？

- What is the extension number for the receptionist?
  櫃臺的分機是幾號？

- I'm sorry. The line is busy.
  抱歉，電話忙線中。

- I'd like to make a collect call.
  我要打對方付費電話。

- May I have that telephone card, please?
  我要買一張電話卡，謝謝。

 由國外撥打電話回台灣，如：（02）2365-9739。

國際冠碼	+國碼	+區域號碼	+對方的電話號碼
如 001（美國）或 000（法國）	886（台灣）	2（區域號碼的「0」要去掉）	2365-9739

1. 一般電話可利用上述方法直接撥電話回台灣。
2. 利用行動電話撥回台灣要看機種。有的不能撥打，有的是與電話公司簽好合約後就可以撥打。
3. 利用公共電話撥打時，要看清楚是否可打國際電話，並需購買國際電話卡。

Supplementary Vocabulary 單字補充

area code	區碼	country code	國碼
dial	撥號	redial	重撥
cordless phone	無線電話	cellular phone	行動電話
local call	市內電話	long-distance call	長途電話
phone book	電話簿	yellow pages	工商電話簿
voice mail	語音留言	answering machine	答錄機
reverse the charge	對方付費	Internet phone	網路電話
ring tone	電話鈴聲	transfer	轉接

Useful Expressions 常用例句

1. Is there a pay phone around here?
   請問這附近有公共電話嗎？
2. I'm looking for a public phone.
   我在找公共電話。
3. How can I make a long-distance call?
   我要怎麼打長途電話？
4. How do I get an outside line?
   我要怎麼撥打外線？
5. May I please borrow your cellphone?
   我可以借用你的手機嗎？
6. Do you mind if I make a short international call on your phone? I will use my phone card.
   你介意我用你的手機打通國際電話嗎？我會用自己的電話卡。

Making Phone Calls 2 （打電話 2）

MP3 

Hello. May I speak to Peter Davison?
喂，請問彼得．大衛森在嗎？

Who should I say is calling? 請問是哪一位找他？

The name is Melissa Kutcher from the Hong Kong Hilton Hotel. 我是香港希爾頓飯店的梅莉莎．庫奇。

I'm afraid you have the wrong number.
抱歉，你打錯電話了。

Jason is not available. 傑森不在。

When should I call back to talk to her?
那我什麼時候再打來比較方便？

Please tell Janet I need to talk to her about the airline ticket. 請告訴珍妮我要和她說機票的事。

Can you take a message for me?
可以請你幫我留言嗎？

Good-bye. 再見。

Useful Expressions 常用例句

May I ask who is calling please? 請問您的大名？

This is Sophie Godwin. 我是蘇菲・高文。

Who are you trying to call? 請問你找哪一位？
I'm calling for Jeffery Bell. 我找傑佛瑞・貝爾。

Can you put Jessica on the line, please?
請問潔西卡在嗎？
Jessica is not in. Can you contact her later?
潔西卡不在家，你要不要晚點再打過來？

Hello. This is Helen Payne. Can I talk to Brian?
喂，我是海倫・潘恩，請問布萊恩在嗎？

He is on another line.
Would you like to leave a message?
他在講另一支電話，你要不要留話？

Hello, reception. How can I help you?
櫃臺，您好。需要我為您服務嗎？
Can you connect me to the Blue Bar?
可以請你幫我轉接到藍調酒吧嗎？
Please hold while I transfer your call.
請稍候，我為您轉接。

76 Mail System （郵局業務）

I would like to send a parcel to Taiwan by airmail.
我要寄航空包裹到台灣。

postcard 明信片	airmail 航空郵件	express mail 快遞
parcel 包裹	surface mail 水陸郵件	registered mail 掛號信
letter 信件	printed matter 印刷品	

mailbox 郵筒	postage stamp 郵票
zip code 郵遞區號	fragile 易碎的
sender 寄件人	addressee 收件人

Where can I find a mailbox?
請問哪裡有郵筒？

How long does it take to send a letter to Japan? 請問寄信到日本要多久？

What is inside the parcel?
這個包裹裡裝的是什麼？

I'd like to have this package insured for $30.
我這個包裹要保險30元。

Two 55-cent stamps, please.
我要買兩張55分的郵票，謝謝。

Supplementary Vocabulary 郵政相關字彙

postage 郵資	postmark 郵戳	mail carrier 郵差
aerogram 郵簡	first-class mail 平信	domestic mail 國內郵件
overseas mail 國際郵件	sea mail 海運郵件	certified letter 雙掛號信
P.O. box 郵政信箱	insured mail 郵件保險	parcel post 包裹郵件

Useful Expressions 常用例句

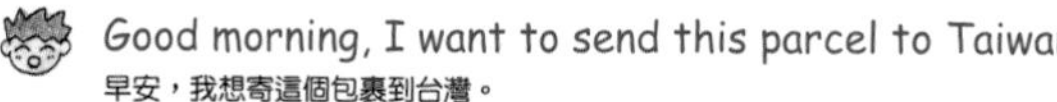

Good morning, I want to send this parcel to Taiwan.
早安，我想寄這個包裹到台灣。

By airmail or surface mail? 寄空運還是一般水陸？

How long would surface mail take? 請問水陸多久才會寄到？

Up to three or four weeks for surface mail.
It depends on the sailing of the ships.
Airmail would take only five to seven days.
通常是三到四星期，要看船運的情況，航空郵件大概是五到七天。

How much would this parcel cost me by airmail?
這個包裹寄空運的費用要多少？

Just let me weigh it for you. That'd be US$35.
我秤一下，總共是35美元。

Thanks. That'll be OK. 謝了，那就寄空運的好了。

Bank （銀行）

MP3 74

Do you have any small change?
請問你有零錢嗎？

change 零錢	coin 硬幣
ten-dollar bill 十元紙鈔	amount 數目

Is there a bank nearby? 請問這附近有銀行嗎？

Do you take visa cards? 請問你們收visa信用卡嗎？

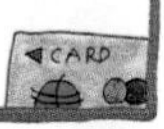

Can you break a fifty-dollar bill?
可以跟我換50元零錢嗎？

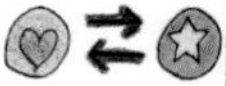

May I see your passport, please?
請讓我看一下護照？

Please sign your name here.
麻煩在這裡簽名。

bank card 金融卡	exchange rate 匯率
traveler's check 旅行支票	checkbook 支票簿

Part 9 日常生活

Supplementary Vocabulary 單字補充

account	帳號	deposit slip	存款單
balance	餘額	safe-deposit box	保險箱
mortgage	抵押	currency	幣貨；通貨
vault	金庫	loan	貸款
bankbook	存摺	withdrawal slip	提款單
interest rate	利率	bank statement	對帳單

Currency 貨幣

1. 美國貨幣單位為 dollar（美金），英國的貨幣單位為 pound（英鎊），縮寫為 £，歐洲目前通用貨幣為 Euro（歐元），縮寫為 €，日本的通用貨幣則是Yen（日幣），縮寫為 ￥。

2. 美元

dollar/buck	$1.00
quarter	$0.25
dime	$1.00
cent/penny	$0.01

3. 英鎊

pound	£1
penny	£0.01

penny（便士）指的是一便士的硬幣；pence則是指 penny 的複數。

 78 Currency Exchange 1 （兌換外幣 1） 

Where can I exchange some money? 請問哪裡可以換錢？
What's the exchange rate between the . . . and the . . . today? 今天……對……的匯率是多少？
I want to exchange these . . . for . . . . 我想把這些……換成……。

NT dollar(s) 新台幣	Vietnamese đồng 越南盾
US dollar(s) 美金	Malaysian ringgit 馬來幣
euro(s) 歐元	
Thai baht 泰銖	
Japanese yen 日圓	
South Korean won 韓圜	

▶ euro 一字在歐洲地區無複數形式，在英語中則有複數形式 euros，請視使用地區調整用語。

Exchange Rates
We Sell
AUSTRALIA
BRAZIL
CANADA
CHINA
Costa Rica
Euro
HONG KONG
JAPAN
MEXICO
NEW ZEALAND
S Korea
SINGAPORE
Sweden
Switzerland
TAHITI
TAIWAN
THAILAND

Dialogue 實用對話

How would you like your money?
您的錢要怎麼換？

1. Please include some small change.
   請部分換些零錢。
2. I would like ten $100 bills, four $50 bills, ten $10 bills, and the rest in small change.
   我要換成十張100元，四張50元，十張10元，剩下的給我零錢。
3. Would you please break this into smaller bills?
   可以幫我換成小鈔嗎？
4. I would like to cash some traveler's checks.
   我要把這些旅行支票換成現金。

Useful Expressions 常用例句

1. Do I need to pay a handling charge?
   請問要付手續費嗎？
2. The amount of money is not right.
   金額錯了。
3. Please sign your name on the checks.
   請在支票上簽名。
4. Could I have an exchange receipt?
   請給我交易收據。

79 Currency Exchange 2 （兌換外幣 2）

U.S. Money 美國貨幣

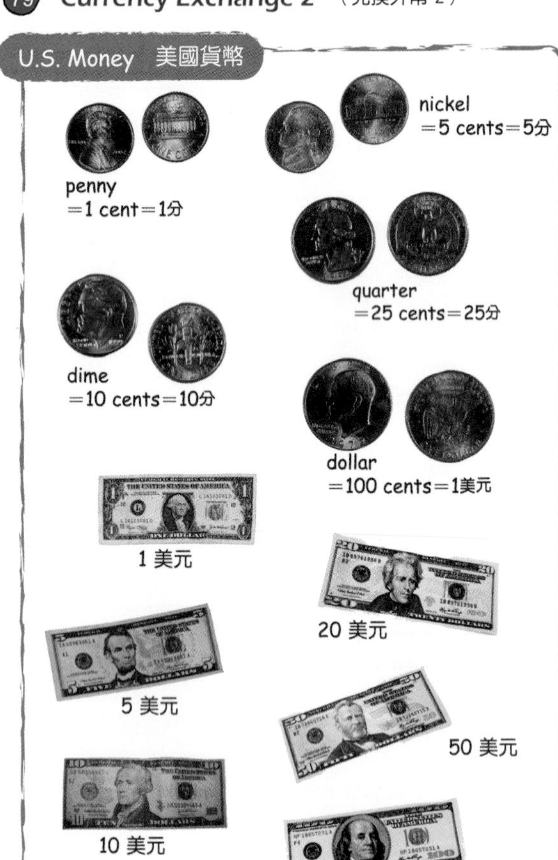

UK Money　英國貨幣

英鎊（GBP），以符號「£」代表，1英鎊等於100便士（pence），簡稱為P。硬幣（coins）面額有1、2、5、10、20、50便士、一英鎊及二英鎊。紙鈔（notes）面額有5、10、20、50英鎊。

1便士　2英鎊　10便士

20便士　50便士

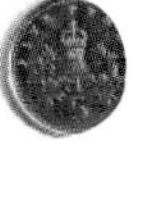

5便士　2便士

1英鎊

80 ATM

MP3 76

Please press 1 to choose a language.
請按 1 選擇交易語言。

Withdrawal 提款	Deposit 存款
Transfer 轉帳	Pay taxes 繳稅

Please insert your ATM card. 請插入提款卡。

Please input your PIN, and press "ENTER".
請輸入密碼後按「確認」。

Please select deposit type.
請選擇存款方式。

Please select the account to be debited.
請選擇轉出帳戶。

Please select the account to be credited.
請選擇轉入帳戶。

Please enter the amount you wish to transfer.
請輸入轉帳金額。

Please press "Enter" to confirm, otherwise press "Cancel."
確認請按「 Enter」，取消請按「Cancel」。

Please take the printed Customer Receipt.
請取出明細。

Dialogue 1 實用對話 1

What are your banking hours?
請問你們銀行的營業時間是幾點到幾點？

From 9 am to 3 pm, Monday through Friday. We are closed on Saturdays and Sundays.
週間上午九到下午三點，週末不營業。

Dialogue 2 實用對話 2

Would you please tell me where I can change some money? 請問我可以去哪裡換錢？

Over there at the Bank of America.
您可以去那邊的美國銀行換錢。

Dialogue 3 實用對話 3

Hello. I'd like to change some US dollars into NT dollars. Could you tell me today's exchange rate?
你好！我想把這些美元換成新台幣，請問今天的匯率是多少呢？

According to today's exchange rate, every US dollar in cash is equivalent to 31.75 NT dollars. How much would you like to change?
今天一美元對台幣的匯率是31.75，您想換多少？

Dialogue 4 實用對話 4

I'd like to break a 100-dollar bill.
我想把這張一百元的鈔票換開。

How would you like your change?
您想要怎麼換呢？

81 Laundry （洗衣店）

At the laundry 在洸衣店

Where is the nearest laundry?
最近的洗衣店在哪裡？

How much do you charge for each item?
每件衣物送洗費用多少？

These items of clothing need to be dry-cleaned.
這些衣服要乾洗。

Could you try to remove the stain on the blouse?
可以去掉襯衫上的污漬嗎？

This piece of clothing cannot be put in the dryer.
這件衣服不可以烘乾。

Could you have it ready by ten this morning?
今天上午10點以前可以好嗎？

When will my clothes be ready?
衣服哪時候會好？

Have you finished my laundry?
請問我送洗的衣服好了嗎？

We charge an extra $5 for urgent cases.
急件要加收5元。

One piece of clothing is missing. Could you look for it?
少了一件，能查一下嗎？

82 Hair Salon （美容院）

At the Hair Salon 在美容院

- Where is the nearest hair salon?
  最近的美容院在哪裡？
- I'd like to make an appointment at two this afternoon.
  我想要預約今天下午兩點。
- I would like to have a haircut.
  我想要剪髮。
- Could you dry my hair?
  可以幫我把頭髮吹乾嗎？
- Please rinse my hair.
  請幫我潤絲。
- How about some hair spray?
  要噴一點定型液嗎？
- Please put some hair care cream on my hair.
  請幫我抹些護髮霜。
- Where do you part your hair? Middle, right, or left?
  頭髮怎麼分？中、右、左？
- How would you like it cut?
  您想要怎麼剪？
- Just a trim, please. Not too much off.
  請稍微修剪一下。不要剪太多。

83 Fixing Items （修理物品）

Where can I get my . . . repaired? 我要去哪裡修我的……？			
	laptop 筆記型電腦		shoes 鞋子
	cellphone 手機		watch 手錶
	camera 相機		glasses 眼鏡

How much is it to have this fixed? 修理這些要多少錢？
How long does it take to fix it? 多久能修好？
Please give me a call after you fix it. 修理好之後，請打電話通知我。
This was damaged beyond repair. 這個損壞嚴重，沒辦法修了。
It's almost seven years old. It isn't worth having it repaired. 這東西差不多七年了，不值得送修了。

 Lost and Found （遺失物品）

MP3 

- Did you happen to see a cellphone here? I lost mine.
  請問你有沒有在這裡看到一支手機？我掉了手機。

- I left my bag in the taxi. What can I do?
  我把包包忘在計程車上了，怎麼辦？
- I think I left my wallet in your shop.
  我的錢包好像放在你們的店裡，忘記拿走了。
- I lost my traveler's checks. May I have them reissued?
  請問，我掉了旅行支票，可以申請補發嗎？
- Could you please describe your lost item?
  可以形容一下失物的外觀嗎？
- I suggest that you report your loss to the police.
  那我建議您向警方報案。
- Please contact me at this number if you find it.
  找到了請打這支電話給我。
- Where can I go to have my passport reissued?
  要去哪裡補辦護照？
- I want to report a lost credit card.
  我要掛失信用卡。
- Could you cancel my card number, please?
  我要將信用卡作廢。
- Can I get a replacement card for now?
  可以申請一張臨時卡嗎？

85 Traffic Accident（交通事故）

It's really awful! There is an accident at the crossroads. 太可怕了！十字路口發生了一起交通事故。

How did it happen? 這是怎樣發生的？

Two buses crashed into each other and 30 people were injured. 兩輛公車相撞，有三十個人受傷。

Oh, that's really awful. A serious traffic accident happened. 噢，好可怕喔。發生了一起嚴重車禍。

You should report it to the police department. 你應該向警察報案。

Did you get the license number of the car? 你有沒有記下那輛車的車號？

Before I realized what had happened, the car was gone. 我還沒弄清楚發生了什麼事，那輛車就跑了。

Useful Expressions 實用例句

1. There was a car accident in Tenth Street this morning. 今天早上在第十街發生了一起車禍。
2. Be careful when crossing the street. 過馬路時要小心。
3. Could you send an ambulance, please? There's been a car accident! 發生車禍了，麻煩您派一輛救護車來好嗎？
4. Don't brake suddenly. The car behind might crash into you. 不要突然煞車，後面的車可能會撞到你。
5. The traffic in this area is so terrible. 這一帶的交通狀況很不好。

Dialogue 實用對話

A: What's the matter? 出了什麼事啦？

B: The road ahead is blocked. There's an accident at the crossroads.
前面的路被堵住了，十字路口發生了一起交通事故。

A: Is there any other way we can take?
還有別的路可以走嗎？

B: No. This is one-way traffic. 沒有，這是單行道。

86 Car Problems （汽車故障）

- My car has broken down. 我的車子拋錨了。
- The engine won't start. 引擎發不動。
- Charge the battery, please. 請幫我把電瓶充電。
- I've got a flat tire. 我的車子爆胎了。
- I had an accident. Please inform my emergency contact. 我出車禍了。麻煩通知我的緊急聯絡人。
- Can you send somebody to tow it away? 請派人來拖吊好嗎？
- Could you have a look at the brakes as well? 順便幫我看一下煞車好嗎？
- The brakes cannot hold well. 剎車不靈。
- The car isn't running smoothly. 車子開起來不太順。
- Nothing serious. I can fix it right now. 沒什麼大問題，我可以馬上修好。
- Do you have a spare tire? 你有備用輪胎嗎？

There is something wrong with the . . . Please check it for me.
……有點問題，可以幫我檢查一下嗎？

	battery 電瓶		engine 引擎
	radiator 水箱		tire 輪胎

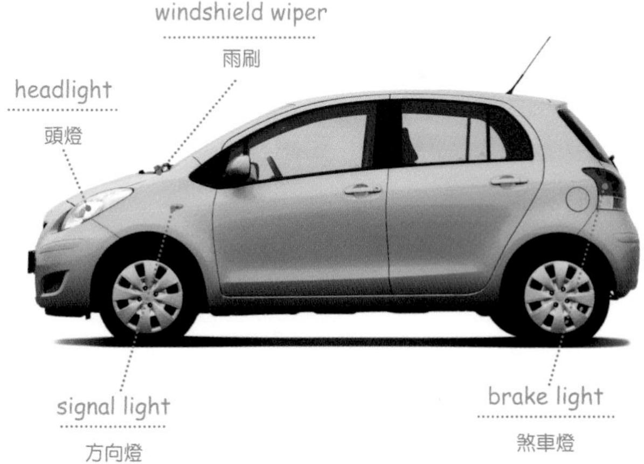

 Having Trouble 1 （遇上麻煩 1）

My wallet is lost. 我的 皮夾 不見了。	My baggage is stolen. 我的 行李 被偷了。	
purse 皮包	clutch bag 手拿包	backpack 背包
pocketbook 小錢包	change purse 零錢包	passport 護照

Help! 救命啊！	Watch out! 小心！
Stop it! 住手！	Thief! 小偷！
Stop him! 阻止他！	Go away! 走開！

Where are we? 這裡是哪裡？

Did you see my son and daughter? 你有看到我兒子和女兒嗎？

Please call the police/ambulance. 請幫我報警／叫救護車。

Does anyone here speak Chinese? 這裡有人會說中文嗎？

I'm sorry. I didn't mean it. 對不起，我不是故意的。

May I use your phone? 我可以借用你的電話嗎？

Supplementary Vocabulary 單字補充

pickpocket 扒手	mugger 強盜	victim 受害者
accuse 控告	arrest 逮捕	catch 抓
prison 監獄	witness 目擊（證人）	bail 保釋
escape 逃跑	guilty 有罪	commit a crime 犯罪

Useful Expressions 常用例句

1. I'd better call the police right away.
   我最好馬上報警。
2. Is that the police station? 那是警察局嗎？
3. I want to report a crime! 我要報案。
4. Can I have your cellphone number?
   可以給我你的手機號碼嗎？
5. We will be there in about five minutes.
   我們大概五分鐘後會趕過去。
6. Be calm. We'll be there right away. 別慌張，我們馬上就到。
7. Could you describe the man for us? 那個人長什麼樣子？
8. Can you remember what kind of clothes he was wearing? 你記起他當時穿什麼衣服嗎？

88 Having Trouble 2（遇上麻煩 2）

MP3 84

the police 警察／警方	emergency 緊急事故	fire engine 消防車

I want to report a car accident. 我要通報車禍意外。

I have been robbed by two guys. 我被兩個人搶劫了。

說明發生地點

I'd like to report a fire at the southeast corner of Garden Avenue and Fifth Street. 花園大道和第五街交叉口東南方轉角上有火災。

說明自己的姓名、電話

I'm Jennifer Hanway. My contact number is 003-196043.
我叫珍妮佛・漢威，聯絡電話是003-196043。

台灣駐外代表處

位置	名稱	住址	電話
美國	Taipei Economic and Cultural Representative Office in the United States	4201 Wisconsin Avenue, NW Washington, D.C. 20016 U.S.A.	(002-1-202) 895-1800
加拿大	Taipei Economic and Cultural Office in Canada	45 O'Connor Street Suite 1960, World Exchange Plaza Ottawa, Ontario, Canada K1P 1A4	(002-1-613) 231-5080
英國	Taipei Representative Office in the U.K.	50 Grosvenor Gardens London SW1W OEB United Kingdom	(002-44-20) 7881-2650
法國	Bureau de Representation de Taipei en France	78, rue de l'Universite, 75007 Paris, France	(002-33-1) 4439-8830
日本	Taipei Economic and Cultural Representative Office in Japan	20-2, Shirokanedai 5-chome Minato-Ku,Tokyo 108-0071, Japan	(002-81-3) 3280-7811
澳洲	Taipei Economic and Cultural Office in Australia	Unit 8, Tourism House 40 Blackall Street Barton, Canberra ACT 2600, Australia	(002-61-2) 61202000

Dialogue 1 實用對話 1

A: Can you describe the man who robbed you?
你能形容一下搶你的人嗎？

B: He's of medium-build and six feet tall.
He was wearing a black T-shirt and blue jeans.
他身材中等，身高大約六呎，穿著黑色T恤和藍色的牛仔褲。

A: What sort of hair does he have?
他的髮型呢？

B: I didn't see much of it. He was wearing a green baseball cap. He had pale white skin and red eyebrows, and he hadn't shaved for a week or so.
我沒看清楚，他戴了綠色的棒球帽，皮膚很蒼白，眉毛是紅色的，還有，他大概一星期沒刮鬍子了。

A: How old is he? 他年紀多大？

B: Pretty young. In his late teens or early twenties.
很年輕，大概只有十幾歲或二十出頭。

Dialogue 2 實用對話 2

A: Did you see the accident happen? 你目睹意外發生？

B: Yes, I did. 沒錯。

A: Was anyone seriously injured? 有人受重傷嗎？

B: No, thank goodness. 沒有，謝天謝地。

89 Illness（常發生疾病症狀）

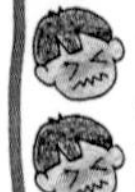

Where is the nearest hospital?
最近的醫院在哪裡？

I don't have an appointment, but it's an emergency.
我沒有預約，可是情況很急。

pharmacy 藥局	general hospital 綜合醫院

flu 流行性感冒	nausea 反胃；想吐
cough 咳嗽	fever 發燒
sore throat 喉嚨痛	diarrhea 拉肚子
running nose 流鼻水	sneeze 打噴嚏
shake 顫抖	stuffed up nose 鼻塞

I don't feel well. 我覺得不舒服。

dizzy 頭暈的	nauseated 想吐的
chills 畏寒	headache 頭痛

Useful Expressions 常用例句

- I have come down with the flu. 我感冒了。
- I have a high fever. 我發高燒。
- I've been suffering from a bad toothache for two days.
  我的牙齒已經痛兩天了。
- I have a really bad headache. 我的頭很痛。
- Nothing will stay down when I eat.
  我一吃東西就會吐出來。

Dialogue 實用對話 - 在診所

A: Good evening. What seems to be the problem?
晚安，有什麼不舒服的嗎？

B: I've got a serious headache and sore throat.
我頭很痛，喉嚨也痛。

A: How long have you had them? 痛多久了？

B: It all started the day before yesterday. 前天開始痛的。

A: I should think you've got the flu. Take some medicine and stay in bed for a day or two.
我想你是得了流行性感冒。你吃點藥，在床上休息一兩天。

B: OK. How do I take the medicine? 好的，那藥該怎麼吃？

A: Just take the prescription to the drugstore. The pharmacist will give you instructions on that.
拿著處方到藥房，藥劑師會告訴你。

B: Thanks a lot. 謝謝。

90 Body Parts （身體部位名稱）

I think my ankle is sprained. 我想我扭傷腳踝了。

This wound is painful. 傷口很痛。

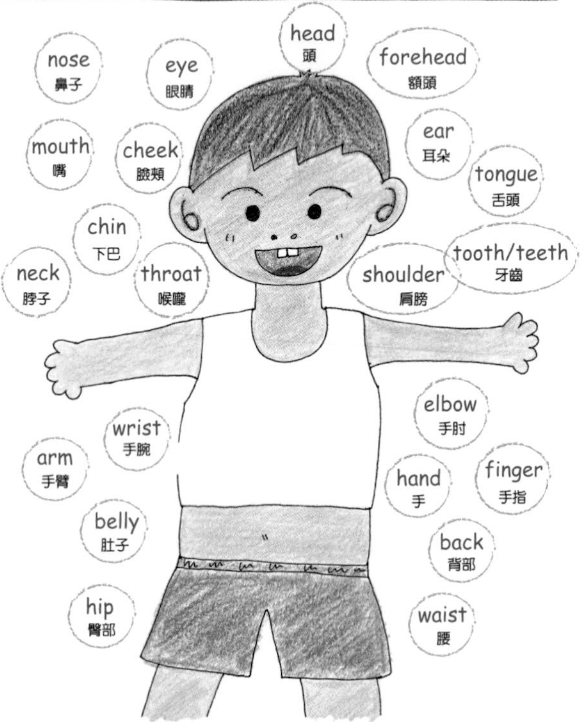

head 頭

nose 鼻子

eye 眼睛

forehead 額頭

mouth 嘴

cheek 臉頰

ear 耳朵

tongue 舌頭

chin 下巴

neck 脖子

throat 喉嚨

shoulder 肩膀

tooth/teeth 牙齒

elbow 手肘

wrist 手腕

arm 手臂

hand 手

finger 手指

belly 肚子

back 背部

hip 臀部

waist 腰

91 Injury & First-Aid （受傷與急救）

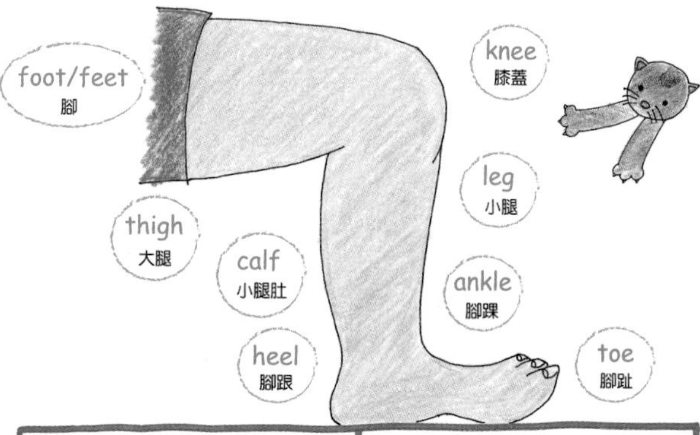

sprain 扭傷	cut 割傷
bleed 流血	splinter 刺傷皮膚的木屑、金屬等
broken bone 骨折	scratch 擦傷
fall down 跌倒	crick （頸或背）抽筋

first-aid kit 急救箱	band-aid OK繃
bandage 繃帶	gauze 紗布
cotton pads 棉片	

92 Body Parts and Organs（手、內臟及其他身體部位）

finger 手指
thumb 大拇指
right hand 右手
index finger 食指
left hand 左手
middle finger 中指
ring finger 無名指
fingernail 手指甲
little finger 小指

bone 骨頭
navel 肚臍
Achilles tendon 跟腱 *
chest 胸部
skin 皮膚
joint 關節
forearm 前臂
underarm 腋下

* 跟腱：小腿接近腳跟的肌肉。

viscera 內臟

brain 腦	lung 肺	
heart 心臟	gullet 食道	liver 肝臟
stomach 胃	large intestine 大腸	small intestine 小腸
pancreas 胰臟	spleen 脾臟	bladder 膀胱
artery 動脈	vein 靜脈	blood vessel 血管
muscle 肌肉	bronchus 支氣管	blood type 血型

93 Skin Disease/Common Disease（皮膚／其他疾病）

MP3 89

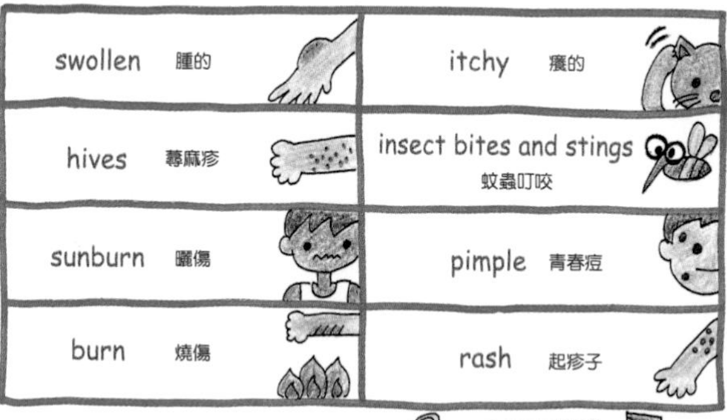

swollen 腫的	itchy 癢的
hives 蕁麻疹	insect bites and stings 蚊蟲叮咬
sunburn 曬傷	pimple 青春痘
burn 燒傷	rash 起疹子

insecticide 殺蟲劑

What do you think it is, doctor? 醫生，請問你覺得是什麼病？	You have the flu. 你感冒了。

food poisoning 食物中毒	stomach flu 腸胃炎
pneumonia 肺炎	heat exhaustion 中暑
tympanitis 中耳炎	appendicitis 盲腸炎
piles 痔瘡	rhinitis 鼻炎

94 Medical Care （疾病／受傷時的說法）

I feel dizzy. I think I'm going to faint.
我頭很暈，我覺得我快要昏倒了。

My throat is dry and sore.
我的喉嚨又乾又痛。

I have a very bad headache.
我頭痛得很厲害。

When will I start to feel better?
我要多少才會覺得好一點？

I am allergic to aspirin.
我吃阿斯匹靈會過敏。

How is your appetite? 你的胃口如何？

My chest hurts every time I breathe.
我只要一呼吸胸口就痛。

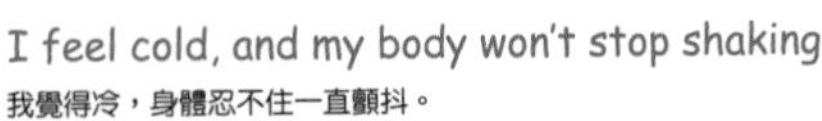

I feel cold, and my body won't stop shaking.
我覺得冷，身體忍不住一直顫抖。

My stomach aches so much that I feel like vomiting. 我胃痛得不得了，我覺得快要吐了。

The wound on my knee hurts badly.
我膝蓋上的傷口痛得很厲害。

95 Medication （藥物）

MP3 

I would like some pills for stomach pains.
我想要買一些治胃痛的藥。

pill	藥丸	tablet	藥片
powder	藥粉	capsule	膠囊
painkiller	止痛藥	cough syrup	咳嗽糖漿
antibiotics	抗生素	aspirin	阿斯匹靈
ointment	藥膏	eardrops	耳滴劑
laxative	瀉藥	eye drops/eyedrops	眼藥水

When should I take the medicine?
什麼時候該吃藥？

Every 4 hours	Before meals	After meals	Before bed
每四小時	三餐飯前	三餐飯後	睡覺前

Are there any side effects?
會不會有什麼副作用？

Do I need to come back again, doctor?
我還要再回診嗎，醫生？

96 Other Diseases （其他疾病）

Have you ever been diagnosed with any of the following conditions?

你曾經被診斷出有以下疾病嗎？

gout 痛風	diabetes 糖尿病
hypotension/ low blood pressure 低血壓	hypertension/ high blood pressure 高血壓
heart disease 心臟病	hepatitis 肝炎
asthma 氣喘	cancer 癌症

When did the symptoms start?

請問症狀什麼時候開始的？

monthly period/ period/menses 生理期	pregnant 懷孕的
anemia 貧血	cavity 蛀牙
allergy 過敏症	

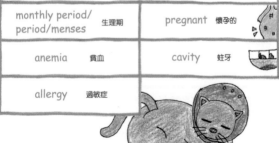

 97 Medicine（醫療相關字詞） MP3 

doctor 醫生 	nurse 護士 

medicine 內科	surgery 外科	ENT (ears, nose & throat) 耳鼻喉科
dentistry 牙科	pediatrics 小兒科	ophthalmology 眼科
obstetrics 婦產科	urology 泌尿科	dermatology 皮膚科

injection 打針	i.v. bottle 點滴
anesthesia 麻醉	X-ray X光
operation 手術	prescription 處方籤
emergency room 急診室	stretcher 擔架

Who should I contact to get my medical report?
請問我要聯絡誰拿我的診斷證明？

I have purchased overseas medical insurance.
我買了海外醫療保險。

98 Self-Introduction （自我介紹）

Hello! My name is Jennifer Young.
你好！我是珍妮佛·楊。

Hi. I'm Dennis Heaton. 嗨！我是丹尼斯·希頓。

Nice to meat you. 很高興認識你。

May I have your name?
請問尊姓大名？

I'm from Taiwan. 我來自台灣。

How old are you? 請問你幾歲？

I'm twenty-seven. 我27歲。

I came here for business purposes.
我來這裡是為了洽公。

I came here to visit a friend. 我來這兒拜訪朋友。

My friend and I are traveling with a tour group.
我和朋友一起跟團旅行。

We're on our honeymoon. 我們正在度蜜月。

Dialogue 1 實用對話 1

A: Could I have your name, please? 請問你的大名？

B: It's Joey, Joey Bennet. 我叫喬伊，喬伊・班內特。

Dialogue 2 實用對話 2

A: Great party, isn't it? 派對真不錯！

B: Yeah, really. 是啊，的確。

A: By the way, my name is Steve Harris.
對了，我的名字叫史帝夫・哈里斯。

B: Nice to meet you, Steve. I'm Eve Marshall.
很高興見到你，我叫伊娃・馬歇爾。

A: Sorry. What's your first name again?
對不起，你說你的名字叫什麼？

B: Eve. 伊娃。

99 Occupation （職業）

What do you do? 請問你的職業是什麼？

I'm a computer programmer.
我是電腦程式設計師。

office staff 上班族	teacher 教師
career woman 職業婦女	doctor 醫生
salesperson/ sales assistant 售貨員	lawyer 律師
bank president 銀行總裁	chef 廚師
student 學生	secretary 秘書
housewife 家庭主婦	bank teller 銀行行員
unemployed 失業中	hair stylist 髮型師
government employee 公務員	designer 設計師
computer technician 電腦技師	manager 經理人
restaurant manager 餐廳主管	retiree 退休者

Supplementary Vocabulary 單字補充

1. 職業

accountant 會計師	vet/veterinarian 獸醫	engineer 工程師
architect 建築師	repairperson/technician 修理工人	mechanic 機械工
receptionist 接待人員	janitor/building custodian 看管房子的管理人員	
agent 經紀人	real estate agent 房地產經紀人	

2. 工作內容

attitude 性向／態度	supervisor 上司	apprentice 學徒
commute 通勤	salary 薪資	income 收入
colleague 同事	employer 雇主	employee 員工
day shift 日班	overtime 加班	promotion 升遷
raise 加薪	time off 休假	sick leave 病假
resign 辭職	pension 退休金	labor union 工會

Dialogue 實用對話

A: What do you do for a living? 你是做什麼工作的？

B: I work for a management consulting company. And you?
我在一家管理顧問公司上班，你呢？

A: I'm a teaching assistant in an elementary school.
我是一所小學的教學助理。

Hobby（興趣）

What is your favorite pastime? 你最喜歡的休閒活動是什麼？	
watching movies 電影	listening to music 音樂
watching TV 看電視	playing poker 撲克牌
traveling 旅遊	playing computer games 玩電腦遊戲
gossiping 閒聊	reading 閱讀
playing video games 玩電視遊樂器	reading comic books 看漫畫書
playing football 踢足球	fishing 釣魚
mountain climbing 登山	making desserts and sweets 做點心
dancing 跳舞	cooking 烹飪

Dialogue 1 實用對話 1

A: How do you spend your free time? 你都做什麼休閒活動？

B: I like watching sports on TV. 我喜歡看電視轉播運動比賽。

A: Are you interested in playing tennis? 你對網球有興趣嗎？

B: Yes. It's one of my favorite sports.
有啊，那是我最喜歡的運動之一。

A: Do you find tennis games interesting or do you also like to play the game? 你是喜歡看網球賽還是也喜歡打網球？

B: Yes, I like both. I would never miss a chance to watch a tennis game. 我都喜歡，我從來不會錯過看網球賽的機會。

Dialogue 2 實用對話 2

A: Do you play bridge? 你喜歡玩橋牌嗎？

B: I've never played it. But I'd like to try.
我沒玩過，不過倒想試一試。

A: You would find it extremely fascinating.
你或許會發現橋牌真的很有趣。

Useful Expressions 常用例句

1. What's your hobby? 你有什麼嗜好？
2. What are your interests? 你對什麼有興趣呢？
3. What's your favorite leisure activity?
你最喜歡從事什麼休閒活動？
4. Which games do you like best? 你最喜歡玩什麼遊戲？
5. How do you spend your spare time? 你空閒時間都做些什麼？

101 Sports（運動）

MP3 97

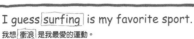

I guess surfing is my favorite sport.
我想衝浪是我最愛的運動。

Basketball is very popular in our country.
籃球在我們國家很受歡迎。

baseball	棒球	swimming	游泳
tennis	網球	table tennis	桌球
football	足球	bowling	保齡球
basketball	籃球	billiards	撞球
golf	高爾夫球	wrestling	摔角
skiing	滑雪	karate	空手道
skiboarding	滑雪板滑雪運動	judo	柔道
marathon	馬拉松	sumo	相撲
badminton	羽毛球	fencing	西洋劍

Supplementary Vocabulary 單字補充

stadium	體育場	arena	競技場	gym	體育館
athlete	運動員	coach	教練	judge	裁判
sporting goods	運動器材	team	隊伍	spectator	觀眾

Useful Expressions 常用例句

1. Ice-skating is really enjoyable. 溜冰真的很好玩。
2. I'm crazy about riding horses. 我熱愛騎馬。
3. I'm a big football fan. 我是個足球迷。
4. My main interest is scuba-diving. 我最大的興趣是水肺潛水。
5. I go for water sports in a big way. 我超級喜歡水上運動。
6. I don't have much interest in boxing. 我對拳擊不怎麼感興趣。

102 Daily Conversation（社交談話）

father 父親	mother 母親	grandfather 祖父	grandmother 祖母	son 兒子
daughter 女兒	brother 兄弟	sister 姊妹	relative 親戚	cousin 表親
uncle 叔叔	aunt 阿姨	nephew 姪子／外甥	niece 姪女／外甥女	dog/cat 狗／貓

Can you give me your telephone number?
可以告訴我你的電話號碼嗎？

email address 電子郵件	address 地址	cellphone number 手機號碼

I'm married. 我已婚。

I'm seeing someone. 我有對象了。

I'm traveling with a friend. 我和朋友一起旅行。

How long will you be staying in New York?
你會在紐約待多久？

It's nice to meet you. 很高興遇見你。

I'm happy to have the pleasure of meeting you.
我很高興有這個榮幸能認識您。

This is definitely a place I'd like to visit again.
這裡絕對是我想再來的地方。

Have you ever been to Taiwan? 你到過台灣嗎？

Please contact me if you come to Taiwan. 來台灣的話請和我聯絡。

Part 12 人際社交

Supplementary Vocabulary 單字補充

ancestor 祖先	neighbor 鄰居	spouse 配偶
husband 丈夫	wife 妻子	in-laws 姻親
father-in-law 公公／岳父	mother-in-law 婆婆／岳母	
half-brother/sister 同父異母或同母異父的兄弟姊妹	stepfather 繼父	
stepmother 繼母	widow 寡婦	widower 鰥夫
generation gap 代溝	adoption 領養	orphan 孤兒

Dialogue 實用對話

A: Are you Carol Delven? 請問你是卡蘿・戴文嗎？

B: Yeah. I'm sorry, you're . . . 是啊，對不起，你是……

A: I'm Mark Hudson. Don't you remember me? We met once in London last summer.
我是馬克・哈德遜。你不記得我了嗎？我們去年夏天在倫敦見過一面。

B: Oh, yes! We met at Buckingham Palace. Glad to see you again.
哦，對啊，我們在白金漢宮見過，真高興又見到你。

103 Blood Types/Astrological Signs（血型／星座）

MP3 99

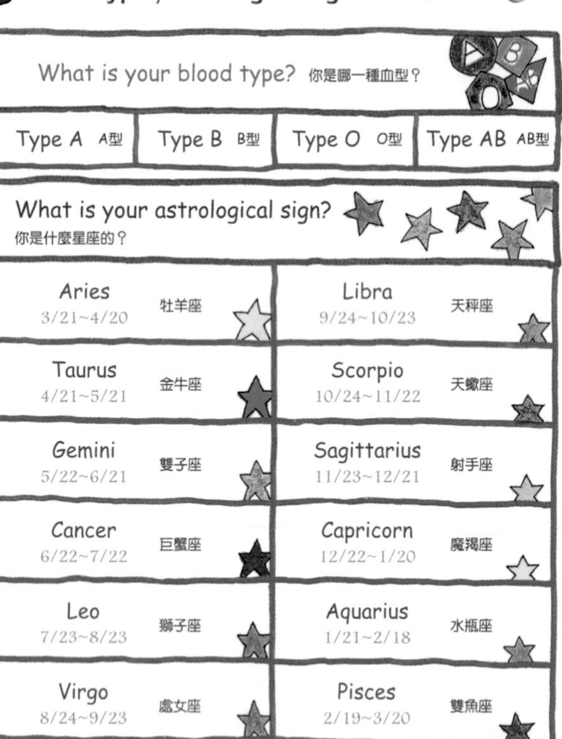

What is your blood type? 你是哪一種血型？

Type A A型	Type B B型	Type O O型	Type AB AB型

What is your astrological sign? 你是什麼星座的？

Aries	3/21~4/20	牡羊座	Libra	9/24~10/23	天秤座
Taurus	4/21~5/21	金牛座	Scorpio	10/24~11/22	天蠍座
Gemini	5/22~6/21	雙子座	Sagittarius	11/23~12/21	射手座
Cancer	6/22~7/22	巨蟹座	Capricorn	12/22~1/20	魔羯座
Leo	7/23~8/23	獅子座	Aquarius	1/21~2/18	水瓶座
Virgo	8/24~9/23	處女座	Pisces	2/19~3/20	雙魚座

What date is your birthday? 你的生日是什麼時候？

Happy Birthday! 生日快樂！

104 Chinese Star Sign （十二生肖） MP3 100

What is your Chinese Star Sign? 你的生肖是什麼？
I was born in the Year of the Rabbit. 我是兔年生的。

Year of the Rat 鼠	Year of the Horse 馬
Year of the Ox 牛	Year of the Goat/Sheep 羊
Year of the Tiger 虎	Year of the Monkey 猴
Year of the Rabbit 兔	Year of the Rooster 雞
Year of the Dragon 龍	Year of the Dog 狗
Year of the Snake 蛇	Year of the Pig 豬

Personality （性格）

What type of personality do you have?
你的個性如何？

I'm a very straightforward person.
我是個很坦率的人。

easygoing	隨和的	energetic	精力充沛的
generous	大方的	stingy	小氣的
friendly	友善的	strict	嚴格的
shy	害羞的	talkative	話多的
humorous	幽默的	boring	無趣的
cheerful	愉快的	unattractive	不好看的
intelligent	聰明的	careless	粗心的
honest	坦率的	rude	粗魯的
kind	親切的	stubborn	頑固的
innovative	創新的	clumsy	笨手笨腳的

Supplementary Vocabulary 單字補充

able 能幹的	mean 刻薄的	lazy 懶惰的
bright 聰明的	introverted 內向的	patient 有耐性的
confident 有自信的	humble 謙虛的	short-tempered 脾氣不好的
conservative 保守的	polite 有禮的	selfish 自私的

Dialogue 1 實用對話 1

A: Tell me something about your best friend.
談談你的好朋友吧。

B: She's slender and she dresses very nicely.
她很苗條，穿著很講究。

A: What else can you tell me about her? 還有呢？

B: She's fun and generous. She's got the best personality in the world.
她幽默又慷慨，個性是全世界最好的。

Dialogue 2 實用對話 2

A: How do you feel about our tour guide?
你覺得導遊人怎樣？

B: I like him. He is polite towards others.
我很喜歡他，他對人很有禮貌。

House Types （住屋）

MP3 

house 獨棟房屋	condominium (condo) 公寓大樓（有產權）
apartment building 公寓大廈	duplex 雙層公寓
study 書房	living room 客廳
bedroom 臥室	kitchen 廚房
bathroom 浴室	toilet 馬桶

How about coming over for dinner tonight?
今晚要不要過來吃個飯呢？

Sure. Thank you for inviting me.
沒問題，謝謝你邀請我。

What a nice house! 好漂亮的住家！

I've remodeled the kitchen and the bedroom.
我整修過廚房和臥室。

May I use your bathroom? 我可以借用廁所嗎？

Dialogue 實用對話

A: Good evening. So, this is your new apartment. It's very nice, isn't it?
晚安！這是你的新公寓嗎？看起來很不錯耶。

B: I like it because it's so convenient. It's only a five-minute walk to the train station.
我很喜歡這間公寓，到火車站只要走五分鐘，很方便。

A: That's great! How many rooms does it have?
那太好了。這間公寓有幾個房間？

B: There are three bedrooms, a large living room, a kitchen, and a bathroom.
有三間臥室、一間大客廳、一間廚房和一間浴室。

A: How are you going to decorate them? 你打算怎麼裝潢？

B: I'm going to paint the walls white, and I'm going to make the curtains tomorrow, and they're going to be green.
我打算把牆壁漆成白色的，明天要做窗帘，綠色的窗帘。

A: It sounds lovely. I'm looking forward to seeing how it all will look.
聽起來好像很不錯，我等不急想看裝潢後的樣子了。

B: So am I. There is an awful lot of work to do before that time. 我也是呀，只是在這之前還有很多苦差事要做。

107 Music（歌唱與音樂）

MP3 

concert 音樂會	encore 安可／加演節目
singer 歌手	dance hall 舞池
band 樂團	microphone 麥克風

pop music 流行樂	rock' n roll/rock-and-roll 搖滾樂
classical music 古典樂	jazz 爵士樂
rhythm and blues (R & B) 節奏藍調	rap 饒舌樂
country 鄉村樂	soft rock 抒情搖滾
hip-hop 嘻哈樂	

Do you know the lyrics to this song?
你知道這首歌的歌詞嗎？

What's your favorite type of music?
你最喜歡哪一種音樂類型？

Musical Instruments 樂器

accordion 手風琴	 flute 長笛	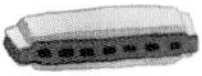 harmonica 口琴	
 cello 大提琴	 music stand 樂譜架	 piano 鋼琴	 guitar 吉他
 drum 鼓	 tambourine 鈴鼓	 keyboard 鍵盤	 trombone 伸縮喇叭
 xylophone 木琴	 violin 小提琴	 trumpet 小喇叭	 triangle 三角鐵

Useful Expressions 常用例句

1. Who is your favorite musician? 你最喜歡哪一位音樂家？
2. Are you a classical music fan? 你是古典樂迷嗎？
3. I want so much to get a ticket to that Jazz concert. 我實在很想要那場爵士音樂會的門票。
4. I've never liked blues music. 我一向不喜歡藍調音樂。
5. I think oldies are more enjoyable than modern dance music. 我覺得老歌比現代舞曲更好聽。
6. I've got two tickets for the pop festival. Would you like to go with me? 我有兩張流行音樂節的門票，要一起去嗎？

 108 Opposite Words（反義詞）

nice 好的
bad 差的

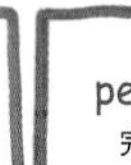

fast 快的
slow 慢的

perfect 完美的
defective 有缺點的

glad 開心的
sad 沮喪的

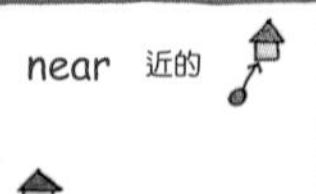

near 近的
far 遠的

same 相同的
different 不同的

broad 寬廣的
narrow 狹窄的

simple 簡單的
difficult 困難的

professional 專門的
amateur 業餘的

quiet 安靜的
noisy 吵雜的

clean 乾淨的
dirty 髒污的

real 真實的
unreal 虛假的

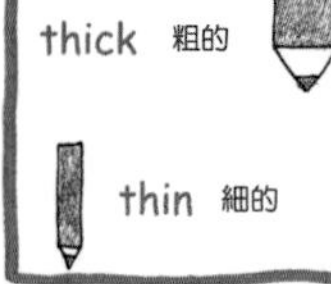

thick 粗的
thin 細的

Dialogue 1 實用對話 1

A: What's the best time of the year to visit the western coast of Florida? 什麼季節去佛羅里達西岸最好？

B: I think summer is the best time. 我覺得夏天去最好。

A: What are some of the things you can do there? 在那裡可以做什麼活動？

B: It's a great place for swimming, sailing, parachuting, shopping and sightseeing. 那裡是個游泳、玩風帆、跳傘、購物、觀光的好地方。

Dialogue 2 實用對話 2

A: How's the weather in Tokyo? 東京的天氣如何？

B: It's really hot in the summer, but it's rather cold in the winter. 夏天很熱，可是冬天很冷。

A: How about in the spring? 春天呢？

B: Quite nice. We have warm clear days most of the time. 春天的天氣很好，大部分都是溫暖的晴天。

Dialogue 3 實用對話 3

B: Have you ever been to the Netherlands? 你去過荷蘭嗎？

A: No, not yet. 沒有，還沒去過。

B: Netherlands is marvelous in the summer, isn't it? 荷蘭的夏季實在太棒了對吧？

A: I'm afraid I know very little about summer time in the Netherlands. 恐怕我對荷蘭的夏季一點也不了解。

附錄

ニャー

出國點檢表

一、基本資料

團名：＿＿＿＿ 伙伴：＿＿＿＿ 旅行社：＿＿＿＿

領隊：＿＿＿＿ 導遊：＿＿＿＿

地點：＿＿＿＿ 時差：＿＿＿＿小時 電壓：110V/220V

國際電話/傳真 外國→我國：＿＿＿＿ 我國→外國：＿＿＿＿

國外緊急聯絡方式：（我國駐當地大使館或代表處、親友等……）

＿＿＿＿

日期：＿＿＿＿ ＿＿年＿＿月＿＿日 到 ＿＿年＿＿月＿＿日

集合時間：＿＿＿＿ 集合地點：＿＿＿＿ 集合時緊急聯絡人／電話：＿＿＿＿

停車地點： 聯絡電話：

機票／訂位代碼：＿＿＿＿ 起飛時間：＿＿＿＿

機票號碼：＿＿＿＿ 回程（當地）時間：＿＿＿＿

再確認日期／時間：＿＿＿＿ 航空公司電話：＿＿＿＿

再確認代號：＿＿＿＿

出國前其他準備事項：

＿＿＿＿

二、必備資料、證件

□ 機票 □ 護照（有效期限超過六個月）、簽證		□ 備用護照用照片（2張）
□ 旅行日程表 □ 地圖（筆、螢光筆：標示路程用）		□ 接機人、電話：
□ 住宿地點電話：	□ 住宿地點傳真：	□ 住宿地點網址：
□ 美金（與新台幣匯率）	□ 外幣（與新台幣匯率）	□ 旅行支票
□ 信用卡（預借現金密碼、緊急救護、特約服務）		□ 海外旅行保險（單）
□ 公出差旅經費額度（$／天）：		
□ 當地消費水準	□ 行李箱鑰匙、密碼	□ 國際駕照

三、用具、工具

- ☐ 手提電腦（隨身碟、光碟機、滑鼠、充電器） ☐ 相機（電池、充電器、其他）
- ☐ 手機（電池、充電器） ☐ 電壓轉換插頭：輸出 _____ W
- ☐ 相機記憶卡 ☐ 萬用插座 ☐ 隨身聽（耳機、電池）
- ☐ 錄音筆 ☐ 計算機 ☐ 旅行用熨斗 ☐ 吹風機
- ☐ 旅遊指南、地圖 ☐ 閱讀書籍、雜誌 ☐ 辭典、外語會話書籍
- ☐ 公事資料： ☐ 公事包、手提包 ☐ 名片
- ☐ 重要待辦事項清單：
- ☐ 紀念品、禮品： ☐ 文具用品（草稿紙、便利貼、筆）

四、衣物、用品

- ☐ 正式衣著（西裝、套裝）：_____ 套 ☐ 襯衫：_____套
- ☐ 正式皮鞋：_____雙 ☐ 領帶（夾）、飾品、領巾 ☐ 襪子：_____雙
- ☐ 其他：
- ☐ 休閒衣服：_____件 ☐休閒長褲：_____條 ☐ 休閒短褲、短裙：_____件
- ☐ 休閒鞋、襪：_____雙 ☐ 拖鞋 ☐ 帽子 ☐ 陽傘 ☐ 輕便雨衣
- ☐ 腰包 ☐ 內衣：_____件 ☐ 內褲、免洗內褲：_____件
- ☐ 襪子、免洗襪：_____雙 ☐ 睡衣 ☐ 短褲：_____ 件 ☐ 其他：
- ☐ 盥洗用具（牙刷☆、梳子☆…） ☐ 毛巾 ☐ 化妝品、香水、古龍水、噴霧水★
- ☐ 生理用品 ☐ 刮鬍刀、刮鬍泡★ ☐ 手帕、衛生紙、（濕）紙巾
- ☐ 針線包☆ ☐ 指甲刀、萬用刀★ ☐ 洗滌用品、洗衣粉
- ☐ 塑膠袋、夾鏈袋 ☐ 小型衣架 ☐ 安全別針、長尾夾
- ☐ 安眠眼罩、耳罩 ☐ 鬧鐘 ☐ 手電筒、防煙（頭／口）罩
- ☐ 運動衣褲、運動鞋襪 ☐ 泳衣、泳褲、泳帽、蛙鏡 ☐ 防曬用品
- ☐ 海灘用涼鞋 ☐ 扇子 ☐ 小水瓶、保特瓶 ☐ 夾克外套、風衣、雪衣

四、衣物、用品

□ 毛衣	□ 衛生衣	□ 圍巾、手套、雪帽、耳罩	□ 暖暖袋	□ 其他：
□ 隱形眼鏡（清潔用具）	□ 太陽眼鏡	□ 老花眼鏡	□ 望遠鏡	
□ 枴杖	□ 助聽器	□ 軟式購物袋	□ 背包	□ 地址、電話號碼簿
□ 採購清單（比較價目）				

☆牙刷、梳子、針線包、撲克牌等可向機上空服人員索取。

★刮鬍泡、噴霧水、萬用刀、螺絲起子等壓縮氣體／液體容器或刀具應隨行李托運，不得隨身攜帶。

五、常備藥品

□ 習慣性用藥：

其他：暈車藥、暈機藥、止痛藥、退燒藥、綠油精、安眠藥、萬金油、胃乳、OK繃、護唇膏、護膚乳液……

六、備用食品、物品

□ 速食麵、杯麵、杯湯	□ 零食：		□ 口香糖
□ 牙線、牙籤	□ 開罐器	□ 保溫水壺、保溫瓶	□ 撲克牌☆
□ 其他：			

七、回程

□ 確認機票、護照	□ 確認到機場的方式、時間	□ 確認採購物品
□ 家中、汽車、行李箱鑰匙、停車卡（隨身攜帶）	□ 備妥新台幣、零錢	
□ 檢查行李箱（物品勿遺漏於旅館中）	□ 檢查隨身行李	□ 備妥機場稅（外幣）
□ 提早Check-out	□ 剩餘外幣（用完、換回、捐出、留作紀念）	
□ 免稅商店大採購	□ 一路順風，平安歸來！	

超簡單手繪旅遊英語 二版

作者 Iris Chang
審訂 Dennis Le Boeuf/ 景黎明
繪圖 橋本友紀／蔡怡柔
編輯 陸葵珍／羅竹君
校對 歐寶妮
製程管理 洪巧玲
出版者 寂天文化事業股份有限公司
電話 +886-2-2365-9739
傳真 +886-2-2365-9835
網址 www.icosmos.com.tw
讀者服務 onlineservice@icosmos.com.tw
出版日期 2018 年 02 月 二版五刷 500201

國家圖書館出版品預行編目資料

超簡單手繪旅遊英語（二版）/ Iris Chang 著 —
[臺北市] : 寂天文化, 2018.02印刷 面； 公分.

ISBN 978-986-318-248-1 (20K平裝附光碟片)
ISBN 978-986-318-410-2 (20K精裝附光碟片)
ISBN 978-986-318-322-7 (32K平裝附光碟片)
ISBN 978-986-318-529-1 (32K精裝附光碟片)
ISBN 978-986-318-660-1 (50K平裝附光碟片)

1. 英語 2. 旅遊 3. 讀本

805.18 107000838

郵撥帳號

1998620-0 寂天文化事業股份有限公司

訂購金額 600（含）元以上郵資免費
訂購金額 600 元以下者，請外加郵資 65 元
若有破損，請寄回更換